In *Love* with Losers

A Novel by LaToya S. Watkins

In *Love* with Losers

A NOVEL BY LATOYA S. WATKINS

Peace in the Storm Publishing

ISBN-13: 978-0-9819631-6-7

Library of Congress Control Number: 2009901142

Publisher's Note

Peace In The Storm Publishing, LLC.
P.O. Box 1152
Pocono Summit, PA 18346
www.PeaceInTheStormPublishing.com

Praise for
In *Love* with Losers

"LaToya S. Watkins is destined for greatness as long as she continues to write with verve and imaginative fortitude ... she doesn't disappoint with *In Love With Losers.*"

~Alvin C. Romer, *The Romer Review*

"Move over Terry McMillian! Not since *Waiting to Exhale* have I gotten this close to such positive black female characters! LaToya Watkins has a dramatic and fresh writing style that keeps you reading. We need more writers like LaToya to bring a golden influence to black literature! Her work and talent is appreciated!"

~Stacy-Deanne, author of *Melody*

"LaToya brings a new twist to familiar characters leaving you lusting for more and making any loser strive to become a winner!"

~Péron Long, author of *Livin' Ain't Easy*

"LaToya S. Watkins hits the ground running with her debut novel *In Love with Losers.* Ms. Watkins gives us an up close and personal look at relationships with the WRONG man. As we see these relationships through the eyes of her characters and their friends, we are not disappointed and their stories were engaging from the onset. Ms. Watkins is definitely one of those up and coming authors we need to keep our eyes on."

~Jacqueline D. Moore, author of *Serving Justice*

Dedication

To my winner, Arnold, because you deserve it.

To Jeremiah, Jordan, and Dymond, because you are here.

To Walter Lee, Kiara, and Jessie B.,

because I will never forget.

Acknowledgements

I would like to thank God for being God.

Thank you so much to my husband and children. I love you for being strong those many days that I was sealed up in the office while you took care of home. I don't know what I would do without you. Arnold, I do believe we complete each other.

Mom (Lydia) for your wonderful support. You are truly an amazing woman of God and you must know that he has smiled on you. Dad (Clyde), thank you for being the model winner. I am so proud of you. My sisters, Nene, Shay, and Tamara. You babysat, critiqued, offered advice, and brought just the right losers home for me to write about. You all have shown me what friendship is truly about. I love you guys! Next to my winner, you are my best friends.

My grandparents, Helen and Leo (aka, King and Queen); my aunts, Janice and Pooh (and Amber of course, for keeping my locs tight); my uncles, Ricky, Gerald, Robert, and Jessie B.; my brothers Chauncey, Clyde Jr., and Branden; and all my cousins and all the kids of my first and second cousins (too many of you to list, so please forgive me). I love you all, and know that without you, I would have nothing to write about.

And thank you Deon Stevenson. Since I was fifteen you have always been in my corner in some way or another. I don't care how much time you didn't have for me, you always went out of your way to make it. Your advice throughout the years has meant so much. I doubt you will ever know how much I look up to you. I love you!

Broderick Stevenson, I am obligated to send a bit of love your way. Thank you for being the BIG brother that I never had, even when you were not able to be here. You have always known how to hold it down and really have a person's back. I promise that just because you are not receiving letters from me, it doesn't mean that I'm not writing (I pray that this book proves that to you). I would promise to write more, but it may be too late for that now, so I'll just say, see you soon bro.

Thank you Ms. Dorothy for being the mother-in-law most women dream about; Lloyd for loving me from the very first day you heard my voice, for having such a tender smile, beautiful disposition, and kind heart; Ms. Oma and Aunt Keeta for your encouraging phone calls and cards.

To everyone at Peace in the Storm Publishing, thank you for giving me this wonderful opportunity. Special thanks to Elissa Gabrielle, you are a woman of excellence.

Thanks to my editor, Kathryn Bianchi. I appreciate the late nights and hard work on everything. Your advice has been and will remain golden.

To all of you who were what I call my test audience (Lil, Janice, Shay, Brother Larry and Sister Kay, etc). You guys deserve acknowledgement for that. You have been down since I wrote my first page.

Thanks to LaTasha Moore for your support as well.

And to anyone I failed to mention by name. I love you, and I promise when I get your finger-shaking letter, I'll get it right in the next book.

Thank you to whoever is reading this for your support. It is greatly appreciated. You are the inspiration for whatever comes next.

Loser—

1. a person or thing that loses *especially* consistently

2: a person who is incompetent or unable to succeed; *also* something doomed to fail or disappoint.

Merriam-Webster Dictionary

ZORA

§

She was tired of the dating and the games. Date after date with loser after loser. She didn't quite understand how the young ladies who opted to skip college and a career to lay down and have babies too early with no financial security seemed to have it made when it came to men. Like her friend Donisha. Donisha had been out there, had babies, and found a good man who loved them all. Did she want him? No.

Zora had gone away to college a few months after she graduated from high school. She kept her head buried so deep in her books until she received her doctorate that she didn't have time for boyfriends. She was no saint; she partied hard in the summer and during her breaks, but she didn't get herself caught up in anything serious enough to distract her from her biggest goal—success. She was hooded with honors in the end, but the end was actually only the beginning. It wasn't until her mission was accomplished that she realized she had no one to share it with.

She let out a soft sigh as she paced in front of the brightly lit classroom while her students took their midterm.

She couldn't help but think—hope even—that Will was the one. She should have seen all the signs in her previous relationship, but she had wanted so badly for the games to be over and for her never-ending chase to end, that she ignored them. For Zora, Will had to be the real deal. She simply could not handle another loser. She thought about the week before—the night she had met Will.

"Zora, girl, those pumps are bad! Where did you get them?" Donisha asked with a look on her face that let Zora know not to take them off around her friend, or they would be gone.

"I got em at that wholesale shoe store on Bentworth Street last year. You really like em?"

"Uh-huh," Donisha replied with a decided look on her face.

"Well sista girl, you working that mini," Zora said with a smile on her face.

Zora checked out Donisha's club attire and laughed to herself at her "hoochie momma" friend. Donisha wore a pleather micro-miniskirt and a glitter baby t-shirt with "Delicious" printed in hot pink letters across her breasts. Donisha was busty after two pregnancies and the word protruded right off of the woman's body. Even with two pregnancies under her belt, she was still the number one money at Brown Sugar. Zora always thought that she had such beautiful chocolate skin and the perfect little almond shaped face. She wore her hair in long micro-braids all the time and wouldn't be caught dead without them. Even now as Zora partied with her heavily made-up, shiny-lipped friend and waited for the rest of the girls to arrive, she wondered how two people so different could be as close as they were.

Donisha went on with laughter in her voice, "Girl, you ain't quite looking like the square I know you to be tonight. You gon git some mad play tonight Zora. Look at you showing that shape."

Zora looked down at herself and knew exactly what Donisha meant. She had picked her orange-colored slacks a little bit tighter than usual, and although she worked hard to keep her body in shape, she didn't like the idea that everyone at "The Den," could see the shape of her perfectly round buttocks. Her burgundy sleeveless shirt was even cut too low and stopped too high for her own liking. She had decided that she wouldn't remove her orange, tight-fitting utility jacket at all that night. The only part of her outfit that she seemed to be comfortable with was the burgundy vintage-styled pumps with the orange butterflies on the side of each shoe.

Pam, her stylist, had out done herself on the bounce in her bob and the bronze streaks she added that morning. They went perfect with Zora's chestnut skin. Pam had even talked her into wearing her contacts instead of her glasses to show her big doe eyes.

"Girl, look at Miss Thang, here she comes now," Donisha interrupted her thoughts. Zora looked up to see Chelle, one of the other members of their female entourage, and her current boyfriend, Ty, being checked at the door.

"Why did she bring him, D? This is our night!" Zora whined. She wasn't supposed to bring her thugged out boyfriend to The Den, and Zora intended to pull her to the side and let her know. As Chelle trotted her healthy body to their table behind her boyfriend, Tyrone, Donisha and Zora exchanged worried glances. How much fun would Chelle be or be able to have tonight with him and his overbearing eyes there?

Ty reached the table first and opened his crushed diamond filled mouth.

"I ain't tryna to spoil ya'll night a nuttin. I'm just dropping Chelle off. Got some biniz to take care of and since I was in the parking lot, I wanted to check out ya'll lit ole spot."

Donisha eyed the odd couple with a curious look on her face before she spoke, "OK, Ty, we appreciate you branging our girl out." She then looked directly at Chelle as if she were blocking Ty out and continued, "But Chelle, what's up with your car?"

Ty chuckled and answered before Chelle could open her mouth, "She don't know, somethin wrong wit that raggedy piece of shit."

"Awight," he spoke again, looking around the club with curiosity in his eyes. Zora couldn't help but think of how amazed that he must have been with the lounge-restaurant style of The Den. The table that they had was right next to the marble dance floor. She could see the bewilderment in his eyes and how he was used to the juke joint holes-in-the-wall that were not so different from Harpo's in *The Color Purple,* except for maybe the shooting and the drugs. Even with all the wooden floor boards and jelly jars for drinks, Zora had failed to see crackheads and dealers in the 1980s movie. But Zora knew that even Harpo's would have been a step-up for Tyrone. He finally turned to walk away but turned back to Chelle as if he had forgotten something. "Oh and I might swang thu, so hit me when you get home," he said while grabbing a handful of her plentiful buttocks.

Zora watched in disgust as the lopsided image of Snoop Dogg disappeared through the doors of the club. Ty reminded Zora so much of her last horrendous relationship with whom she considered to be the biggest loser in the world, Bryan Thompson. She blamed Bryan for her inability to find love. She just didn't understand why she always attracted such losers. She was an intelligent, young, African American sista with credentials in education that any "smart" man would be proud of. All she seemed to attract were thugged-out buffoons. At twenty-nine years old Zora had sworn off men. She wasn't into women or anything like that; she just didn't have time for the games that men played. She was beginning to think that she was one of the people that God had chosen to walk the walk alone—like Apostle Paul.

She turned her head and looked at Chelle. She admired her full face and dreamy eyes. Chelle was an absolute thick beauty. Her skin was the perfect shade of chestnut and her eyes were almonds that any man would get lost inside. She was the product of an interracial marriage. Her father was African American, and her mother was Japanese. Chelle carried about 165 pounds on her five-foot, one-inch frame, but she wore it all so well. She had wide hips like her mother and a big butt, probably like her father's mother. Zora just didn't understand her attraction to Ty.

He was a honey complexioned guy with thick coarse hair that he sometimes wore braided, but most of the time when Zora saw him it was loose all over his head. He was not tall at all, about five foot, eight inches at most. His two front teeth were both gold and slightly bucked. It looked to Zora like the brother was trying to hide a serious gap. He wore a semi-neat goatee, and his beady little eyes made him look sneaky. He dressed like a thug with no money before Chelle, but Zora had noticed that recently his white Ts and jeans looked a little more expensive, and he was always sporting new kicks. To Zora, he was a loser with a capital "L." Chelle had a great future ahead of her, and in Zora's eyes, she was putting it all on the line for Ty.

"Chelle, girl why didn't you call me? I would have picked you up," Zora asked with true concern as soon as Ty was gone.

"Thanks Zora, but I didn't know that anything was wrong with my car until I went to start it up. It turned over, but it sounded weird, so I just left it at home. Ty was there, so I just told him that I need a ride here." She wouldn't look directly at Zora. Her eyes seemed to hit every place in The Den except for Zora. Zora knew Chelle too well, and when her eyes became shifty, something was wrong. Chelle looked toward Donisha, the drinker in the crew. "What we drinking on tonight, girl?" Zora could tell that Chelle was trying to get off the subject so she just let it go and made a mental note to find out later what was really going on.

"I know that's right," Donisha piped in looking toward the bar. "I'm a go git me a Crown and Coke. You want one?"

"I'll go with you," Chelle replied in an effort to get away from Zora's curious glare. Zora made her request for a Cape Cod and cranberry juice as the two women glided to the bar.

She sat looking toward the door, still soured by visions of Ty, when she saw the sexiest brotha walk in. He was at least six feet, two inches tall. He had a regal yet familiar look. Zora found herself staring at him and judging his grooming. He was on point. He wore his hair cut low but not so low that you didn't notice the curly ringlets. His upper body was covered in a striped button down shirt over a white t-shirt. His jeans were the perfect fit, and from where she sat the whiskered fade was on hit. His skin was a mahogany brown, and she could see his thick lips from her chair. His eyes held a slant that led her to believe that the familiarity that she noticed was from an African tribe, seas away from America. When their eyes locked for a moment, she turned her head.

"He's a far cry from Ty or Bryan," she thought out loud.

"Hey trick, what are you doing sitting here by yourself?" Zora turned to see Kyla and Jamie standing behind her.

"Bout time ya'll made it," she commented with a playful frown as she looked them both up and down.

"Uh-huh, Ms. College Professor Nedham, don't go there," Kyla began, "Some of us aren't privileged enough to only work Monday through Friday. Girl, Peter been getting on my nerves all day. I just shook his ass bout an hour ago."

"Oh yeah, I guess that's the small price you pay for the luxury of being a private nurse. How is Peter doing?" Zora asked. All of the girls knew Kyla's patient Peter. She was a nurse to AIDS patients who didn't want to spend their last days in hospitals. She made good money doing it and had no problem spending it as quickly as she made it. Peter was one of Kyla's patients, but he didn't have AIDS. He was HIV positive, and his family—mainly his father—cut him off socially, because to them the contraction of such a "horrid" disease threatened the status of their socially advantaged family. They did, however, supply him with a generous payoff to stay away from the family, and in addition to the rather large lump sum, he received a stipend each month like clockwork. It was their way of letting him know they cared, but he used most of the money they sent him monthly to hire Kyla.

"He's fine, girl. Where them other bitches at?" Kyla answered Zora's question about Peter, catching a warning look about her language from Jamie, the good girl of the group. Kyla didn't notice the look Jamie had shot her and had she noticed, she would not have cared. She had a bar none attitude and would let whatever she felt like saying slide through her juicy lips. She wasn't as cute as the other girls, but her feisty attitude and brains got her far with the fellas.

"We right here, skeezer," Chelle replied, walking toward the table with Donisha close in tow.

"All right now, that's what I'm talking about," Kyla shouted grabbing the absolute and cranberry juice from Chelle's hand and taking a sip before handing it to Zora. "I'm on my way out to the dance floor," Kyla said as she sashayed to the floor with her four friends close behind.

Donisha was the best dancer in the group, and Jamie had the least amount of rhythm. Donisha wiggled her body like a snake across the dance floor and was quickly followed by a handsome guy that was turned on by her seductive moves. The rest of the girls danced together as their moves were less provocative than hers.

They had been dancing for an hour nonstop, and Zora was glad when someone was bold enough to admit that it was time to go. "Girl, it's time to shake this spot," Chelle yelled over Bob Marley's "No Woman, No Cry."

"Yeah, you're right," Kyla added, "But you ain't fooling nobody. We know you just trying get back to that nigga, but gone and git you some ding-a-ling 'cause I know I'm getting me some. They all erupted in laughter, and that's when Zora felt him grab her hand.

"Excuse me, Miss. Can I talk to you for a minute?" When she looked up, it was the guy from the door sounding just like Jay-Z, and she didn't hesitate to go to him.

"You were the first thing that I saw when I came in here tonight, beautiful, and I need you to do one thing for me," he began with a smooth African accent and a very sexy baritone voice.

"Oh no he didn't," Zora said to herself. He was fine but that alone didn't give him the thumbs-up for requests. She studied his milky smooth skin and tried to avert her eyes from the pink lips that she so badly wanted to touch.

He continued, "My name is Will, and I would like for you to tell me yours when you call me later on tonight." Zora just stared at him. She hadn't been hit with that line before, and she wanted to wait and see what would erupt from his luscious lips next.

"Now you don't have to say a word right now, Ms. Lady. I really want for you to call me; make me wait sweetheart." He handed her a business card that she didn't look at, because she was staring at him and the lips that those bold words had escape from. He touched her chin and said, "I'm leaving right now and heading to the house to watch the phone. If you and your voice are as sweet as you look, you're definitely worth the wait." He turned on his heels and walked away as Zora stood watching his back as it disappeared through the doors of the club.

Zora looked up to see her girls slithering their way from the dance floor with knowing looks on their faces. She looked down at the card in her hand and read it. It gave his name and numbers—home, office, and cell—and all his credentials.

"Who was that fine brother, Zora?" Chelle questioned.

"Can I git me one ah dem?" Donisha asked with a laugh. Zora read the name on the business card before answering, "The name is Dr. William Jameson, ladies, and if one of you wants this damn card, you can have it," she said holding the card out for the girls to take.

Donisha looked at her hand before saying, "hold onto it Zo, I got a feeling you might change your mind on this one."

Zora dropped Donisha off first, because she lived in the low-income housing apartment complex near The Den. When she was alone in the car, she decided to ask Chelle about what was really up with Ty bringing her to the club. Chelle was the youngest of the group, and even though Zora was only two years older than her, she felt the need to look out for her.

"OK Zora, but you better not tell Donisha or Kyla, because I been hearing enough negative crap about Ty from them heffas," Chelle said with an uneasy frown.

"You know me, Chelle," Zora replied, taking her eyes off of the road to look Chelle in the eyes for only a second, "I'm no blabbermouth." Zora knew by the look in Chelle's eyes that she was about to get an earful, so she lifted her heavy foot up off the gas and slowed down her Lexus truck in an effort to lengthen the ride to Chelle's apartment.

"Well," Chelle began, "last night after I took Ty out to dinner to celebrate his birthday, he stayed over. About two this morning my phone rung, not my cell phone, not his cell phone, but my home phone, Zora."

Chelle looked at Zora seriously.

"I answered quickly, because I didn't know who it was. You know how that is, Zora. I didn't know if it was one of the guys calling from the law firm. Sometimes they call pretty late if they get a lead on something; you know how lawyers like to run their paralegals back and forth across the city." She smiled a little bit, and Zora reacted with a soft smile that told Chelle to continue.

"Ty ain't with men calling no matter what." She paused again, and her face expression turned serious again. "Girl, when I picked up the phone before I even said hello, I could hear the chick talking mess to someone in the background, and when I did say hello girl—," She cut herself off and looked out the window.

"Anyway Ty said that he had called his baby momma while I was in the shower last week, and that's how she got my number. Girl, she called me a bitch and told me to put Ty on the phone, and he didn't even get onto her or anything. But anyway, she was cussing and screaming over the phone about him not coming through to see his son Little Tyrone on his birthday."

Zora looked at her and asked, "It was his son's birthday too, Chelle?"

"Yeah, Little Tyrone has the same birthday as Big Ty. He turned two yesterday, and Vonita got mad at me and told him she was on her way over there to kick my ass. I mean, I know Ty's my man, but it's his responsibility to take care of his child, because I don't have any. I didn't know it was his son's birthday, anyway. Me and Ty only been dating three months. Anyway, she came I guess an hour later, but I didn't know until he woke me up telling me that she was outside with her crew dumping candy bars into my gas tank, Zora." She looked out of the window again and then back at Zora.

"I don't even know how the hell she knows where I live, Zora. Ty says that she must have followed him before, but I don't know what to believe."

"Ohhh Chelle," Zora exhaled with sympathy, "I told you when you met him that he reminded me too much of Bryan. That hustler mentality that they have going on overrules any good that these guys have inside. When they live by that code, sadly—it's the only thing that matters. Believe me, I learned the hard way, and sooner or later everything he's doing will catch up to him. When fooling with any man, sweetie, look out for you and only you. You can feel their pain, but you can damn sure feel yours more and that's all that matters. Protect you."

Zora looked at her hand on the steering wheel before adding hesitantly, "And I would hate for you to have to suffer for his mistakes like I am for Bryan's. Anyway, that thug-type guy played out when we were in high school, Chelle. They're losers, and we're too good for them."

Chelle smacked her lips but still kept an even tone. "I know what Bryan did to you Zora, but believe me, Ty is nothing like that. His circumstances made him a thug, and he's gonna grow out of that, I'm sure. I really like him. I think I may even love him, Zora. Just support me in this relationship."

Zora pulled into a parking space next to Chelle's car, looked over at Chelle, and held up her fist, "OK, but I only bring this stuff up because I love you, Chelle, and I don't wanna see nobody hurt you. As bad as I hate to see you with Ty, if them heffas come back you better call me. Me and the girls will be here to whoop ass before you even have time to hang up the phone."

Chelle smiled a grateful smile and wrapped her arms around Zora. "Thanks Zora, and for what it's worth Bryan messed up. He really didn't realize just how lucky he was to have you." Chelle opened the door, and Zora watched until she disappeared into her apartment.

She made it to her house fifteen minutes later and was greeted by her barking poodle, Gideon.

"Hey there, Gideon," she said reaching down to rub his head. Gideon had been Zora's mother's feisty poodle before she was killed with her father in a fire two years earlier. Zora had been distraught and had it not been for Bryan, and the additional support of Donisha, Kyla, Chelle, and especially Jamie, she would have never made it through that trying time. Gideon and the house that her parents left her were the only real family Zora had left. She thought about her parents every day, but her small circle of friends kept her life busy and almost full.

She dropped her keys on the end table in the living room and walked over to the bar that connected her closed off kitchen to her living area. She saw the message light blinking on her machine. She pushed the play button and listened to whoever was on the phone hang up after the beep.

The next message was from Chelle telling her "thank you" again. The fact that the only thing that had been waiting for her at home was her dog and a message from a friend that she had just left was very disappointing to her. Deep down inside Zora wanted a love life, but more than that, she wanted a family. She wanted a message on her machine from a guy, a good guy who wanted to love her and let her love him.

She pulled the card that Will had handed her out of her pocket and looked at it. She picked up the cordless from the base and dialed the cell phone number that was on the card.

"Hello," the baritone voice on the other end answered.

"Hello, Will?" Zora asked.

"Aw, hey Miss Lady. I'm really glad that you decided to call. I guess you do believe I'm worthy of knowing your name."

Zora was impressed with how he remembered her and that increased her curiosity to find out what Dr. Jameson found intriguing about her.

"My name is Zora Nedham, and it is very nice to meet you," she responded in a raspy voice.

"Well Zora—can I call you Zora?" he asked before continuing.

At that point Zora knew that this guy was not going to stop impressing her with his polite mannerism. None of the guys that she had ever dealt with had asked for permission to call her by her first name.

She found out a lot about Will during their three-hour phone conversation. He was a single, thirty-six-year-old man, and his best friend was his brother. He came from a close-knit family from East Africa and had strong family values. He and his brother had been in America for a decade in pursuit of education and careers that would one day earn them enough money to bring their family to the States. He had completed his medical residency a year ago and was still a rookie in his field. He told Zora that since he'd accomplished his dreams career-wise, he was ready to find his wife and fulfill the dreams that he had for a family.

By the time they got off of the phone, they had a date set for the next night at Zapeta's, one of the most expensive Italian restaurants in the city. Zora was still a bit skeptical about dating again, but she figured that one date wouldn't hurt anything.

That was just last week, and now Zora wondered if Will would be the real deal, or if he was about to take her on a one-way ride to Loserville.

CHELLE

§

Chelle couldn't believe what Tyrone was saying to her. Here he was upholding his skanky baby momma after she had tried to sabotage her brand new Volvo by putting Snickers bars in her gas tank.

"Baby, she was just upset about me forgetting my little man's birthday." He had the nerve to be slouching on her couch acting as if she was getting on his nerves.

"Ty," she began, trying to sound like she wasn't mad to avoid a full-blown argument. "I only asked you to tell her not to call here and stay away from my house. Baby, I understand that she was upset, but that does not excuse the fact that what she did was very childish and ghetto."

Chelle watched as his expression changed from boredom to anger. "Hold up now Rachelle, everybody ain't privileged enough to have a daddy for a doctor and a momma that plays that symphony shit. That is the mother of my kids, and I ain't about to let you and nobody else disrespect her by calling her ghetto." He stood up and walked toward her and when he spoke again the bass and anger was gone from his voice.

"Chelle, understand. While yo' folks was buying you ponies and horses for yo' tenth birthday, she was rummaging through dumpsters looking for dinner. When you were graduating from high school and getting ready for college, Vonita was hustling to come up with the money to bury her mother, because she had died from AIDS. That girl done had a hard life. Her momma was a crackhead, and she ain't never known her daddy. She'll never know the beauty of this life that you have known." He gently stroked the side of her face and pushed her soft hair behind her ears.

She looked into his eyes and felt guilty for all the hurt and pain of his past. She felt sorry for Vonita by just looking into Tyrone's eyes. He could relate to her, and he understood her pain. Chelle wanted that with Tyrone so badly, but he kept treating her like his bad life was her fault.

"I know, baby," she began meekly. "I just thought maybe her absence would keep the drama out of my life. I don't have room for these kinds of worries. I'm in my last year of law school, and I'm not willing to jeopardize or compromise that for anything."

He wrapped his arms around her and began to rub her back. "Chelle, don't get me wrong, I'm not saying that Vonita wasn't outta line, but I put her back in her place, and we won't have anymore of those kinds of problems."

He placed his thick soft lips over hers and began to kiss her passionately. He began to lift up her skirt and squeezed her cheeks roughly and tenderly at the same time. She was happy that they had resolved their little problem, so she unzipped his pants and decided to teach him about foreplay; because that was an area that Ty was most definitely lacking in.

When Chelle woke up from her nap after midday sex with Ty, he was gone. She tried not to be pissed about him not waking her up, because whenever she got an attitude with him in the end she just ended up feeling guilty about it. She knew that he was very much aware that she had needed him to drive her to the Volvo dealership to get her car, but something important must have come up. She could just call Zora to come and drive her to the dealership. It was hot outside anyway, and Ty's old Oldsmobile Cutlass didn't have air conditioning.

She stood in her bedroom and looked down from the open loft view into her contemporary furnished living room in search of her cell phone. When she located it resting on the iron glass end table that her parents had bought her, she walked toward the spiral staircase so that she could see whose calls she had missed.

Chelle picked up her phone and flipped it open and noticed that it wasn't hers at all. The screen saver on the phone was a picture of a naked lady, and Chelle knew that she hadn't taken it. Ty was always going to strip clubs and had probably snapped the photo there. She had bought Ty a phone to match hers last weekend because his credit was all jacked up and she wanted to be able to contact her man when she needed to. She looked at the received calls screen, and there were seven missed calls. She knew she shouldn't but she looked to see who had called anyway. The first three missed calls were from "my boo," the second three all said customers; letting Chelle know that he was still selling drugs and lying to her about it. The last call didn't have a name attached to it, but Chelle knew that the area code was close to Donisha's area—the Projects.

She smiled when she scrolled through the calls from "my boo," knowing that it was her, and then she thought about it and didn't remember calling his phone recently. She hit the select button to view the number. It was the same number that was on her home phone the night of Ty's birthday. His boo was his baby's mother.

Chelle was pissed, but there was no way she would say a word to Zora or any of the girls for that matter. She wiped away the silent, private tears that were now sliding down her cheeks and picked up the cordless phone that was lying on her couch. She called Zora and asked her to come and take her to pick up her car. Zora was stoked, because she wanted to talk about her new beau, Will. They made plans for Zora to come over at three, and they would get her car and then go back to Zora's and put some steaks on the grill.

It was one o'clock when Chelle got off the phone with Zora, so she took a long shower and then walked around her bedroom looking for something to wear as she dripped on her hardwood floor until her naked body was dry. She put on her Noni lotion that she stayed stocked in from the Noni man. It had a botanical garden smell that she was absolutely in love with. She had chosen a pair of cream-colored linen Capri pants and a white tank top to wear for the day.

She played with her wild whiskered haircut and applied her lip gloss and eye shadow. She misted herself with the new Gucci scent and went downstairs to wait for Zora.

She walked over to the CD player on her dresser and pushed the power button. Kemistry immediately began to drone about love calling and there being no place to run from it. Chelle became angry with herself while she listened to the male vocalist. She wished she could run from being in love with Tyrone. Deep down inside, she knew that he was no good for her. She had started to miss school and even found herself slacking on her clerkship at the law firm where she worked. Her Aunt Mattie had once told her that negative people create negative energy in your life and that that negative energy can be strong enough to destroy you.

She didn't want to leave Tyrone a note letting him know where she was, she didn't want to call her cell phone either. She really didn't want Ty to use the key she had given him to get back into her house. At that moment, she hated that she had even given it to him. She had told him to let himself in while she was at school one day last month, and he had held on to the key without mentioning it again. She couldn't forget he had it though, because he used it every chance he got.

She knew that he would be there as soon as he realized that he had her phone. She slipped his phone into her Michael Kors bag as soon as Zora knocked. She would just go along with his little slipup and see where the day took them.

DONISHA

§

Donisha sat at the table in Goodie's Kitchen, a hot new Southern-style restaurant, looking at one of the most handsome men that she'd ever gone out with. He looked better than her oldest child's father, and she knew that his money was legal; which was something that she was in no way used to. His hazel eyes blended well with his honey colored skin. She admired the way he wore his hair closely cut, which made it impossible to tell if he had coarse or kinky hair or what some folks call good hair. His facial hair was so neatly trimmed and looked good, but Donisha felt that you never could measure the grade of the hair on a man's head by the grade of the hair on his face.

His name was Marcus Black—Minister Marcus Black. He was far from Donisha's Saturday night date, but she was really feeling him. She had formally met him at her Aunt Glodine's wake two weeks ago, and he didn't hesitate to ask her out after he found out that her mother was the late Bishop Raines's wife. He told her when he first met her that "any daughter of the late Bishop's sure can be a wife of mine." She thought it presumptuous of him to assume her to be worthy of him because of who her father was, but everyone did it.

Everyone thought that just because she was raised in the Raines house she was supposed to be the model of purity. Her father was a real man of God, and everyone in the city knew it. Donisha had three older brothers and one older sister that had all managed to follow the straight and narrow, but she was the apple that fell far from the tree.

Contrary to what everyone believed, Donisha had had her battle with all kinds of street demons. Donisha's other siblings were much older than her. They were so much older in fact that by the time she was born they were all grown and out of the house. With her being the only child at home and her parents being so old, she grew up spoiled and pretty much did as she pleased.

She took the power and the privilege given to her by her parents and dropped out of high school to run away with a drug dealer. She came back home five months later pregnant, and the good Bishop let her stay only when she agreed to complete a GED program. It broke his heart to have to put her out again six months later when he found her snorting coke in the bathroom. He wouldn't let her take baby D'Edward with her to live on the streets, but Donisha had to go.

She stayed with her baby's father for a month before she came running back home. Big D'Edward and Donisha took to snorting coke frequently, and he would tend to go upside her head after they were both good and high. He would bring other women into the raunchy apartment when Donisha was high and try to get her to perform sexual acts with them. When Donisha would protest, he would fight.

The good Bishop was on the porch with his shotgun in hand when D'Edward came to reclaim his woman, and Donisha was looking out the window when he limped away with a bullet in his leg. That was one thing about the good Bishop. He didn't take mess from anyone. He was an upright and well-respected man, and anyone who didn't see that from the beginning found out one way or another.

After that Donisha got a job as an exotic dancer at a local club called Brown Sugar. Her father didn't approve of her career choice, but she had straightened up her act and started taking some classes at the community college. She had even stopped smoking pot and snorting coke. That's when she met Franko.

Franko was an Italian criminal justice major, and he was a pretty good guy. She met him in her English class, and at first they just shared notes when one of them was absent. After the first semester of school, she didn't have classes with Franko, but they started to meet up at the student union for lunch or study time. They were fast friends but slow lovers. Once they did hook up, it surprised Donisha that Franko wasn't nervous about meeting her father. It also surprised her that her father liked him, but everyone she knew got along well with Franko.

His grandparents were Italian immigrants. His family started out in New York when they arrived in America. After Franko's grandparents died, his mother and father moved to Texas. His father dreamed of opening an Italian restaurant but believed that the competition was too big in New York. His father worked hard to start his business but never achieved his goal. He had a gambling problem and took out the wrong loan on a bad race and was murdered for it. Franko's mother moved back to New York to be with her sisters after her husband was killed, but she joined him in death only a few short years later. When Franko told her he was alone in the world, Donisha offered her family to him.

Franko would come over for dinner on Sundays after church and listen to the good Bishop reiterate to him what he spoke about. It amazed Donisha that her father never came down hard on Franko about not attending church services. When Donisha's father decided that he wanted to knock out the wall in the master bedroom to give his wife a bigger closet, it was Franko who came over every day for three months straight and helped her father with the job.

Franko was different from D'Edward, and sometimes his politeness and sensitivity threw Donisha off. He would open doors for her, and he never allowed her to spend a dime of her own money when they went out. He didn't like her dancing at Brown Sugar, but he didn't call her names like

D'Edward did when he found out she was dancing there. Franko was so good with little D'Edward that the baby would run to him whenever he was at the house. Donisha swore that he thought Franko was his daddy. Franko had goals and dreams for a future, and Donisha knew that he didn't see her as a fling or just a sex partner, because he always included her when he talked about his future.

When Donisha became pregnant after five months with Franko, she didn't tell him. She broke up with him and didn't go back to school the following semester. Franko was sick after the breakup. He had fallen in love with Donisha, but she knew that she couldn't bring another child into the world at that time in her life. She had strong feelings for Franko, but the timing was all wrong. She had expected her father to hit the ceiling when she told him and her mother she was pregnant again. He was so hard on her at times, and most of those times she knew she deserved it. Years after her father's death, she still cried when she thought about his words after her guilt-ridden confession.

His weary, wrinkled, and tired face stared into hers longingly. Bishop Paul Raines was a handsome man. His six-foot frame could be intimidating to some, but not Donisha. His salt-and-pepper-colored hair gave off a certain air of wisdom that made lesser men step back and stand down to his authority. But the day Donisha told him she was pregnant again, he was different. He wasn't some wise, strong flock leader; he was daddy.

"Baby, this here life ain' gawn neva be easy. Ole Satan gotta keep us on ah toes." He paused and looked back at Donisha's mother.

"Me and mother dear had high hopes fo ah baby girl. You was the one who was gawn make us proud. What I mean—what I mean to say is, we awfully prouda all ya'll. We just had so many dreams for you."

He paused again and then shocked Donisha when he gently placed his calloused palm on her cheek and let it rest there a while. It must have been strange for him. He had never been an affectionate man. Donisha could not even recall ever seeing her parents embrace each other. He dropped his hand and looked at it as if it felt different after touching her face.

"God laugh all day at ah lit dreams don't he?" He smiled like a father doting on a child who had done a good deed. "Had a little talk wit Jesus. He prepared me for this moment. It's all in his perfect plan. We all fall short, and I know what you wanna do, but it ain't what God wants. He gon turn all this around and work it out for you, lit bit." Donisha hadn't heard him call her by the pet name he had given her since her freshman year of high school.

"You might not understand it today, tomorrow, maybe not even next year. But one day, you'll get it. You will."

Her father talked her out of an abortion, and she stayed inside the house for five months. When she gave birth to the little girl, she didn't even bother to name her let alone look at her. She gave her up for adoption when she was born, but her mother thought it was wrong that Franko didn't know. Needless to say, she called and told him everything. By the time the baby was four weeks old, the adoption had been reversed, because his signature was nowhere on the paperwork and DNA testing had proved that his consent was needed.

Franko took damn good care of his daughter. In fact, she lived with him. He had forgiven Donisha, but she hadn't forgiven him for stopping the adoption. He named their daughter Frankie. He would bring baby Frankie by once a week to see the Bishop, his wife, and little D'Edward. He said a person needed family. All of his family was gone, and it was important to him that his daughter had hers. The Bishop liked Franko even more after that. He said that he was as good a man as God makes. They would talk for hours about God and heaven. Franko was one of the only men that Donisha knew who didn't go to church every Sunday and still chilled with her father on a regular basis. Finally Donisha came around, and she would play with Frankie when she was about a year old. It had become hard to ignore the cheerful baby's presence. She was the cutest baby that Donisha had ever seen. She looked exactly like a union of

Donisha and Frankie. Some people said she was the spitting image of the Bishop. That comment always made him beam with pride. Donisha's feelings were nowhere near the same for Franko's daughter as they were for her son, but she felt that as long as little Frankie had her father, she didn't really need her.

Now she sat across the table from Marcus. She thought about the last words her father said to her a year ago before he died.

"Lit bit, I want you to know that I love you, and I'll always be with you. I always have been proud of you, but I want you to do something to make ya daddy's chest rise." He smiled at her and looked off to some faraway place. "Baby, I want you to make amends with that boy. You can't go on in life until you do. He done a godly thing, and I'm just as proud of him for taking care that child as a I am of you for having her. God ain't gone allow you walk through another door while that one still open. And you remember little angel, God makes no mistakes. Every mistake you think you made, he still loves you and love forgives. You'll get it; I promise, you will." Donisha nodded her head and wiped away the tears that were running down her face. "Stop all that now girl, I'm going home, and next time I see you my chest gon be so big cause you gon make it rise with pride."

She had accepted Marcus's offer because of her father. He would be her link to God. Her link to her father. She had never done anything that her father could brag about, and she knew it. She was going to make him proud.

ZORA

§

The relationship began as sweet as a summer's breeze. Will would stop by with dinner on a nightly basis and stay till the wee hours of the morning. On his first visit, Will was thoroughly impressed with the décor of the house.

Zora's parents had been gone two years, and the day after they were buried she'd packed up her apartment and moved back home.

She hadn't changed a thing about the house since her parents died except for the fact that she slept in the bedroom that they once occupied. She wished that she had the nerve to remove the brass swan and the peacocks that covered the walls of the living room and replace them with pictures and the sculptures of Africa that she had been admiring at the African bazaar. But she knew that removing them would be eliminating pieces of her mother and father. Her mother had decorated the room herself, so to Zora the living room was her mother, or at least a part of her. Some days she missed them terribly, and often she felt like she'd always been a parentless child. They had been a small but close-knit family. Her parents were country folks and knew what it meant to be a family. They taught Zora about family and love and how important having those two things in life is, but now they were gone.

At times she felt blessed to not have been in that fire. Other times she felt cursed for being left alone. Her parents had started taking frequent romantic getaways after Zora left for college, but every so often they'd make it a family affair and take Zora with them. Their last getaway didn't include her—in fact, she had not even known about it until the two officers knocked on her apartment door. Her life changed that day, but back then she had Bryan to soften the blow. He had caught her when she almost passed out from the news. He wrapped his arms around her shoulders and stayed there when she went to identify the almost completely burnt bodies. He soothed her with his melodious words and songs as she cried instead of slept those first few nights. Now even Bryan was gone.

Zora missed her parents. They had been her life, and finding a new one after them was still proving to be a challenge. Zora hoped and prayed that Will was real; she was tired of being alone.

Zora lounged on the sofa of a rented suite. Will had called her the night before and asked her to come by the Embassy Suites where he was staying for the night. His brother was entertaining a guest at the house, and he said that he was too tired to party with them, so he'd just rented a room. Zora had been impressed when he called saying that he wanted her company at the hotel.

Donisha had called earlier, asking Zora to attend dinner the following weekend and to bring Will, so that they could meet each other's significant others. Donisha had started to date some minister, which was weird to Zora because she was anything but a minister's type.

"So what do you think, babe?" Zora asked as she watched Will from the couch while he moved around the kitchen as he fixed their glasses of wine.

"Well, Zora, you know my schedule," he began, "just leave room for something to come up." He started over to

Zora with the glasses in his hand, and a red flag went up for Zora.

"Will, I've told you about how important my friends are to me. I don't have any real family left. Why don't you want to meet them?"

Will handed her one of the wine glasses before sitting down next to her and answering her question, "Zora, it's not that I don't want to meet your friends. It's just that women can be so damn judgmental, and I don't want anything or anyone trying to come in between us before we have a real chance." He looked at Zora with pleading eyes, "Understand where I'm coming from babe, please. Let's just wait a while for that."

Zora looked at him thoughtfully, "I understand, Will, and you can have all the time you need," she said, truly understanding his fear of her friends. She slid closer to him so that she could touch him. When she did that, he automatically slid his arm around her small waist and lowered his head for a kiss. She obliged him and kissed his soft lips and decided to give him all of the passion that she had withheld from him the past weeks. She gently pushed his body against the back of the sofa and could tell by the way he fell back into it that he knew what time it was. She mounted him slowly and made sure that she sat her womanly mound directly on top of the hard part that she could see through his jeans. When Will moaned, she knew that she'd boarded the right place. He moved his hips beneath her as she gyrated in his lap until he finally pulled his lips away from hers.

He looked in her eyes and asked, "Are you ready for this, baby?"

Zora didn't say a word; she just leaned back in and put her lips on his neck and began to unbutton his shirt so that she could taste all of him. "I take it you are," Will moaned as he leaned his head back and closed his eyes. Zora unbuttoned his shirt and began to kiss his chest, taking him away to ecstasy.

Zora left while Will was still asleep. She still couldn't believe how wonderful it had felt making love to him. He was a master pleasurer as his tongue knew no boundaries. She could have lain next to him all day gazing longingly at his sleeping form in one long, deep moment of nostalgia. Zora had promised herself that she would save her body for the man that she would marry one day, but it was hard to keep a man without giving herself to him. When Will had whispered in ear last night what he would do to her if given the chance, she had surrendered her body to him. How she wished she could have stayed in bed with him all day.

But she had to get home and let out Gideon and make sure he had food in his bowl. As much as she was falling for Will, Gideon's well-being was still more important to her than anything in the world. Gideon was the only living thing Zora had left from her parents. Her mother had loved that little dog. Her mother had loved anything that her father gave her, and Gideon had been one of the many gifts that her father presented to his beloved wife.

Zora felt a tinge of guilt during the short drive home. Her mother was a huge advocate of saving sex for marriage. Since her parents' deaths, Zora had tried to honor them in ways that she hadn't while they were alive. Zora's mother had been bedridden her last few years of life, but her father didn't let that stop them from leading a normal life together.

Claude and Mary Nedham were real love. Zora knew that, and she was sure it was why she longed to have that type of love so badly. Yes, they had their problems, but they always overcame obstacles in their marriage. When Mary had to go into the hospital for a hysterectomy a couple of years after Zora was born, Claude was supportive. Mary developed a cyst a year after Zora was born. When the doctors attempted to surgically remove it, they found that it was made up of bone matter, indicating that the mass had once been a fetus. After obtaining consent from Claude, the doctors decided that it was best to clean up everything on the inside so that this would never happen again.

Claude ignored the stories and warnings from some of his friends and coworkers at the fire department about how a woman who had to go through such a major operation wasn't a complete woman at all. Claude and Mary had both known the risks of childbearing, and they had been prepared to face whatever came afterward.

A few weeks after her surgery, Mary was up and about and almost completely back to normal, doing everything from laundry to chasing Zora around the house. During the sixth week of her estimated recovery period, Mary collapsed while cooking dinner. She was diagnosed with multiple sclerosis (MS) that had been triggered by the hysterectomy. Although the doctors had little hope for Mary's survival as her lungs began to fail, Claude refused to give up. He and his two-year-old daughter practically lived at the hospital with Mary. At times Mary grew tired and felt that she was burdening the family. She would make pleas to him, crying, "let me die, this is too much for you." But Claude would just smile at her sadly and say, "You are my life, darling. You ain't going nowhere without me."

He willed her to live and took out several loans on their home to have it updated to fit his handicapped wife's needs. After six months, Mary was released from the hospital, and she entered the care of Claude and the many therapists who all held the common goal to coach her to walk again. Claude's job was big. Mary had tons of medications that Claude had to administer daily. She also had catheters that he had to learn how to change and raging hormones from her recent hysterectomy. But he stuck by her side. After she realized that no matter the condition of her body, her husband was with her for the long haul, she surrendered to forever with him and fought to survive.

The therapy and sheer will to live helped Mary walk again with the use of a cane. It wasn't until the last two years of her life that her legs began to ache so terribly that she could no longer handle therapy, and they failed her once more.

When Mary was unable to walk again, Zora's father retired from the fire department and became his wife's sole caregiver. He took her on trips and showered her with love and affection. When Zora would tell him jokingly, "Daddy, you spoil her rotten," he'd reply with a smile, "Baby girl, I ain't letting yo mama leave this here earth witout me. 'Sides, you never know what a person needs in this life to survive, and I think our girl in there deserves a little spoiling right about now."

Zora's father loved her mother for thirty years, and no matter how intense her health issues became, his love never failed her. Zora's mother once told her that she hadn't done anything to deserve that love, but God saw fit to bless her, and she wanted Zora to understand the importance of waiting on God. Her mother hadn't been very religious before her sickness, but she said that God showed her how good he was by blessing her with such a good husband. Zora would never forget the conversation that her mother started before she left for college. She and Zora were in Zora's room packing for her departure when her mother sat down on her bed. Zora had thought her mother was just taking a rest. The MS was hard on her body, and sometimes she would be in pain and fail to tell Zora and her father. They had to learn to read her body language, and her father had been the master at it.

"Zora," she began, "I want you to try and save yourself honey."

"Huh?" Zora was confused. She had no idea what her mother was referring to. They had talked about sex when she was fourteen, so Zora wasn't expecting another conversation about it. Zora stopped folding the clothes that she was neatly preparing for the many boxes that were scattered throughout her childhood suite.

"Wait for the one God sends." Her mom looked pained and tired; so much until Zora took a seat next to her on the bed.

"I met your father my sophomore year of high school," she went on with a smile. "He had to have been the sweetest guy in the whole school. He was a transfer from some ole country school, you know?" She eyed Zora, but she really didn't expect an answer. "Your father was a short guy back then. He had a wavy Afro, but that was about all he had that a girl my age wanted to look at. He wore Steve Urkel glasses, and his pants didn't fit much better," she giggled. "But he was a sweetheart. He had been too shy to tell me that he wanted to go out with me, so I just saw him as a friend. I was in love with Thomas Jenkins; he was the captain of the football team. He was quite the hunk, and all the girls wanted him, but Thomas only showed interest in me. Or so I thought." A smile spread across her lips, and she leaned closer to Zora as if she was telling her a secret. "Some people got a way of making folks feel like they the only person in the world. Yo daddy like that too, but the difference tween him and Thomas, is yo daddy always meant it. Back then girls played hard to get, so I let Thomas chase me just until I thought he'd quit. After he caught me, we went out the whole year. He was chasing other girls right up under my nose, but I was too in love with the loser to see it. So what did I do? I gave up my most precious gift to him. My virginity." She looked down into her lap, and I knew that she was trying to stop tears from welling up.

"He dumped me the same night. He didn't even stick around long enough to find out about the baby we made together that night, and I didn't tell him about it when I found out six weeks later either. To make a long story short, Claude was the only person there for me. He tried to talk me out of the bathroom abortion that I let the cousin of one of my girlfriends perform on me, but I didn't listen to him." She sighed and stood up holding onto her cane.

"Zora, God has a mysterious way of working things out. I don't think it was an accident that it was so difficult for us to conceive you, nor do I think it's an accident that I walk on this cane. God made me for your father, and I lay down with another before my time. Save yourself, honey. I'm sure he got somebody out there for you. Don't give it up for a loser; save yourself the trouble."

As she thought about that conversation with her mother, all Zora could do was grip the wheel tighter and whisper, "I'm sorry, momma."

Her cell phone rang, and she adjusted her earpiece.

"Hello," She sang into the mouthpiece.

"Hey girl, where you at?"

"On my way to the house, Kyla. Why? What's up?" Zora asked.

"Uh huh, you sound too happy, girl; I'm on my way over there. I'm coming from Michael's mother's house, and I want to stop by there on my way home." Kyla was smacking her gum loud into the phone, and it was annoying Zora.

"I'll be there in few minutes," Zora began, "How far are you? And stop smacking that damn gum!"

"I'll be there in about fifteen minutes; I gotta get something to eat. And listen to this," Kyla started smacking as loud as she could before Zora closed her phone.

Zora laughed at how goofy her friend could be as she pulled onto her street. She noticed a moving truck parked a few houses down from her own home and grew worried. Since the Abbots had moved to Florida after their retirement, their house had been up for sale. "They musta finally sold the place," she thought out loud. Zora knew that there was no telling who was moving into her predominantly white neighborhood.

The last new people on the well-kept block had moved into the corner five-bedroom house across from Zora about a year ago. Zora met them when they were moving in and they invited her to their housewarming party on the spot. They were nice enough and close to Zora's age. Stacy and Karen looked so much alike that Zora automatically assumed that the two were sisters. They were both tall, model-thin redheads with similar smiles.

She had walked into their backyard on the day of the party, and there sat three women lounging in the soft green grass as naked as the day they were born. When she turned her head in embarrassment, there were her new neighbors in the corner of the yard getting it on. Apparently Zora's new neighbors were putting on a live show for their naked audience. Stacy had her head buried so deep in between Karen's legs that Zora thought about rescuing her, but that probably would've gotten her hurt. Karen was beneath Stacy's face humping up and down and moaning in complete delight. When one of the guests saw Zora standing there staring in awe at the spectacle the hosts were putting on, she held up her finger and seductively beckoned Zora to her. Zora turned and fled from the backyard in a hurry after that scene and made it a point to always wave at them from a distance. She had no problem with her lesbian neighbors. They weren't noisy and caused very little trouble, but Zora had no desire to attend any of the wild sex parties that they sometimes threw.

Zora noticed a black man lifting boxes and carrying them from the truck. He had to be one of the movers; if not, his family would be the only other black family on the block. She made a mental note to bake a pie and drop it off later in the week. As she pulled into her drive, she noticed that the guy had put his boxes down and was headed her way. She climbed out of the car and greeted him with a pleasant "Hello."

"Hello," the man said smiling and showing off a very small gap, but otherwise perfectly straight teeth, "I saw you pass by and well—. I guess it excited me to see one of us. My name is Emory Hernes, and I'm your new neighbor." He extended his hand out to Zora, and she accepted it with a shake.

"I'm Zora Nedham," she replied giving Emory a quick glance over. He was OK looking, but he was no Will. He was about Will's height with skin the color of cinnamon and a lean frame. Emory had thin lips but the prettiest green eyes that she'd ever seen. The thing that she liked most was his hair. It was a natural brownish-gold color with neat little locks all over. "I was just making a mental note to bring you a pie once your family was settled in."

"Oh," he replied sadly with lowered eyes, "Just cut a slice out and save the rest for your own family. I don't have a family. It's just me. I'm recently divorced."

Zora immediately felt stupid for putting her foot in her mouth. By the look in the poor guy's eyes, his divorce had hurt him. "Well," she finally stammered after about five seconds of uncomfortable silence. "I apologize about your divorce," she decided to throw in a little something extra to make up for her stupid remark, "Maybe you can stop by for a slice of pie and coffee sometime. It's just me as well."

"That would be great," he said with bright eyes, "Well, I guess I'll get back to work. It's always nice to meet a friendly neighbor, and whenever you get that pie and a bit of free time, feel free to knock on my door and let me know."

She extended her hand to him, and he shook it good-bye. Zora waved good-bye to her new neighbor, and as soon as she stuck her key in her front door, Kyla drove up in her Envoy blasting the latest Usher hit.

Once inside, Kyla threw her keys on the coffee table and dashed to the bathroom while Zora let Gideon out. She filled his dog bowls with food and water and waited for Kyla to come out of the bathroom. As soon as Kyla walked out of the bathroom, she kicked off her pumps and her mouth started moving full throttle.

"OK girl, tell me what's up with Chelle? She been trippin, and I know she told you. You called last week and at least let us know that you wouldn't be at The Den, because you was wit cha man—which by the way does not excuse you from our night. But she didn't even call, and Jamie said she saw Ty leaving some chick's apartment when she dropped Donisha off last night."

Zora looked at Kyla surprised at how long she could go on moving her mouth without taking a single breath. Zora had long given up gossip and shook her head, "Kyla, I really don't know what's going on, but she'll call one of us sooner or later if she needs us." Zora wanted to hurry up and change the subject, "So, how's Mike?"

Zora wasn't particularly fond of Kyla's boyfriend. He seemed nice enough the few times Zora had met him and was definitely what she would call eye candy. His mocha chocolate skin was perfectly smooth and his sexy bedroom eyes were enough to make any woman wanna drop her drawls. He kept his hair cut in a low college trim, and Kyla told Zora that the guy was a shopaholic, a super high-maintenance shopaholic, which was why Zora had such a big problem with him. He was an ex-con, an educated ex-con, but in Zora's mind, an ex-con was an ex-con. He had only been out of the federal penitentiary for a year when Kyla had met him, and even though he had been straight up with Kyla about his situation, he still didn't seem right to Zora.

Mike claimed that love was his biggest crime. He had met some grad school chic who worked part-time at a local bookstore. She had taken it upon herself to steal the credit card machine from the job and bring it home to her sexy mocha man. He was a grad student himself at the time, and he was in need of cash to maintain his lavishly fly lifestyle. So he sold the machine to a guy who got caught and of course ratted him out. Mike's situation had thrown Zora. He came from a two-parent suburban home and had access to the best schools and everything else that any successful guy had. Kyla credited his prison time and the stigma that he had to deal with afterward to a foolish mistake. Zora didn't flat-out call Mike a loser, but she kept her eyes and ears peeled for evidence leading to a loser in Kyla's report of Mike.

"Girl," Kyla glowed at the mention of her boyfriend's name, "He is as busy as ever. I was telling him today that after one year I have yet to spend a whole weekend with him. I guess that is the price I have to pay for having an entrepreneur as a man." She smiled as she pulled back her shoulder-length hair so that Zora could see the diamonds that sparkled in her ears. Kyla was a far cry from what normal people call pretty with her big eyes, overly thick lips and long, narrow face, but she could be a top model with her slender, tall frame. "He gave me these this morning."

"Those are beautiful," Zora sang, "Maybe if I stay on my game I can have some of those soon." After being released from prison, Kyla's boyfriend had a hard time finding a job with his new criminal record. He had recently teamed up with an old friend and started a new party promotion endeavor, but Zora was sure that the little gig wasn't bringing in the cash that Mike told Kyla it was. He lived at home with his parents and drove around in a 1981 BMW that had been completely sanded and had not paint on the exterior at all. Zora silently thought that he would never get his own place if he kept showering Kyla with the expensive gifts he tended to give her. In Zora's opinion, he seemed to care for Kyla enough, but there was a certain boyish approach to his life that bothered her.

"You better get more than these. Mike is a self-proclaimed party promoter, but Will is a doctor. He better come with a lot more than some diamond earrings."

Just mentioning Will made Zora want to call and make sure he had recovered from their midday rendezvous. "So what's up for the rest of the weekend?" Zora wanted to know if they had another weekend outing or if they were just going to wait until Thursday for their ritual happy hour.

"Nothing really. Jamie was gonna go with me to check on Peter. "

Zora hadn't been surprised when Kyla stopped working as an operating room nurse and became a nurse for AIDS patients. When Zora first met her, Kyla was in love with a guy that she called her "African king."

Kyla had met her so-called king, Aky Tecali, after high school graduation. Instead of letting Kyla attend the traditional trip to Cancun, Mexico, with the rest of her senior class, Kyla's parents made her go on a missionary trip with her uncle to Somalia. Kyla left the United States kicking and screaming and returned madly in love with Aky. Six years of love letters and five visits from Kyla to Aky and Aky to Kyla later, the AIDS virus consumed Aky, and he lost his life to the disease. Kyla was there to hold his hand with unquestioning eyes and love in her heart when he took his last breath. It was virtually impossible for Kyla to tell her friends about everything she and Aky went through, from the miscarriage of a baby that they named Akylina to Aky's last breath. But they understood her decision to care for others who suffered the way Aky did.

Kyla only had two patients. Most of her time went to Peter, but there was also Gail. She had full-blown AIDS, and Kyla worked with her through Easy Going Hospice Care. All of Kyla's friends had met Gail and felt bad about her condition, but their visits provided a huge amount of awareness about their own sexual practices.

Gail, who had once been supermodel tall, thin, and gorgeous, had contracted HIV from her fiancé (her high school sweetheart) when she was twenty-four. Over the entire course of their relationship, he was having unprotected sex with other women. Gail never slept with him without a condom, but it wasn't because she was afraid of contracting STDs. That was the furthest thing from her mind. She told Kyla that the only reason she had insisted on using protection with her future husband was because she had not wanted to become pregnant before they were married. She contracted the disease from oral sex with him. Gail was quick to tell Kyla during her rants and raves about not wanting children, "Kyla, there are worse things that you bring home than babies. Believe me, I know."

Gail's fiancé shot himself in the head after he found out he was HIV positive, only leaving behind a letter to let her and six other women know they needed to be tested. Gail had only been intimate with one man in her life, and now he was dead and she was dying. Now, Gail was frail, with open sores covering her body and crusted lips, confined to a bed for the rest of her life.

While Gail had a supportive family and only needed Kyla to come out for an hour or so three times a week, Peter didn't. He didn't need a nurse either. He was living fine with HIV; he took good care of himself. The poor guy just needed a friend, and Kyla did a wonderful job being one.

“Girl, he is so funny,” Kyla continued. “He called saying that he doesn't feel well, but Peter ain't dying, Zora. He thinks I'm stupid. He's just bored as hell. That's all I got planned. Mike's busy tonight as always, and since everybody's gotta man, I'm stuck with Jamie." They both laughed at the joke. Jamie was gorgeous, but she only dated Jesus. They always laughed at the fact that their friend was so holier than thou, and she held a crucifix to men. Jamie had gone through a lesbian stage of her life, and even though she didn't date women anymore, she said that she would probably never date another man. They all knew that her feelings toward men didn't come from nowhere; they had long ago decided to let her talk about her issues when she was ready.

They continued to chat for another hour before saying their farewells.

As soon as Kyla was gone, Zora dialed Will's number. Zora hung up thinking she had dialed the wrong number when a woman answered on the first ring. When she called back and the same woman answered, she went ahead and asked for Will.

"No," the voice said on the other end. She had a deep husky voice and didn't sound very feminine, but Zora was sure it was a woman. "Will is not in at the moment." The women simply ended the call by hanging up. No good-bye, leave a message, or anything. Zora was pissed. She paged Will on his two-way and tried his cell. His voice mail picked up on the first ring on his cell phone, so she just had to wait until he called her back.

Every thought that could possibly pass through her mind did while she waited for him to call back. She dismissed them all though. There had to be a real good explanation for this. Will was educated and successful. He was too smart to be a loser.

"Who in the hell was that woman?" Zora thought aloud as she paced her living room waiting for Will to call back. After ten minutes of that she finally went to run her bath water, taking the cordless phone with her. How could she have been so stupid? She hadn't been out of bed with him for twenty minutes and he had someone else there. The phone rang, and she hit the talk button before it could ring twice.

"Hello, Zora? This is Will. What's up?" He questioned her in a busied tone that only added fuel to the fire.

"Who in the hell was that woman who just answered your phone Will?" She kept her voice straight so that he wouldn't sense her frustration.

"Huh? What? Oh you mean Gloria, my cleaner. Oh, so she did arrive today," he said with a chuckle, "Late as usual. I left my cell phone at home when I stopped by earlier. She must have answered for me. I'm glad you decided to call after you snuck off and left me this morning."

"Oh," was the only response that Zora could make. She was beyond embarrassed, "Well I just wanted to hear your voice. Could you stop by when you leave there?"

"You know I will. Do you need me to bring anything," he asked with laughter in his voice.

"No," she replied meekly, "Just you."

After taking a long nap, Zora woke up and checked her caller ID to make sure Will hadn't called. There was no way she would have heard him knock as hard as she slept. She didn't want to call again, because she'd already said too much the first time, so she just decided to have her own private waiting party on her front porch. It had been three hours since she spoke with Will, and she had no idea how long he would be at the office. She grabbed a stack of test papers and a pitcher of tea and headed for her porch swing.

Karen was in her driveway across the street stretching for her daily run and waved excitedly when Zora emerged from her front door. "Long time no see neighbor," she yelled across the street, "How are you?" Zora knew that Karen was referring to her avoidance since the little housewarming incident. Zora made sure that Karen didn't sense the annoyance in her voice when she yelled, "Oh, I'm fine, and you?"

"I'm good," Karen replied still stretching. She paused like she wanted to say something more, but when she looked back at her house she changed her mind. Zora noticed a nervous smile spread across Karen's lips as she waved good-bye.

She jogged down the drive and started down the block, occasionally looking back at her house.

Zora shrugged and looked down the street to see Emory struggling alone with his couch and decided to be neighborly and lend a helping hand.

"Hey, looks like you could use some help with that," she said as she approached her new neighbor's driveway.

Emory dropped the end of the couch that he was trying to lift and diverted his attention to Zora. A playful frown appeared on his face and he replied, "I guess I do need help even if it is just from a girl." They both laughed, and Zora gave Emory a hand with his couch.

The couch was the last thing on the truck, and after they finished, they took a seat with a couple of beers in hand.

"So neighbor," Zora began, "why were you moving all of that stuff yourself? What happened to friends or moving companies for that matter?"

Emory shook his head and took a sip of his beer before replying, "Well Ms. Zora, for starters I left all my friends in New York. And the movers, well let's just say that I had to fire them, because they kept breaking stuff."

~~~~~

"New York, huh? Wow! What brought you here? I mean coming from up there to Texas is quite a jump."

Emory took another sip of his drink before setting in on the shiny hardwood floor next to his foot. "When my wife and I decided to split up, I realized that I hated my career. I went to law school, but I never really wanted to practice law at all. I come from a family of lawyers, and I guess in my family, law school is just what you do. I left a very prestigious firm in Manhattan because I want to … ," He paused and looked at Zora thoughtfully, "Well, I want to save the world." He smiled as if he were realizing that for the first time in his life.

"I want to travel to poor countries and help out however I can. Practicing law doesn't give you much time for that, but I could use the knowledge that I gained from law school to do what I can for others who don't have it elsewhere, I guess." He paused again. Zora noticed that this guy didn't just blurt things out. His words came from deep thought. She liked that. "When I'm not out trying to make God smile by healing this ole ravaged world, I wanna be here writing about the people that I encounter. So, I guess I'm here to live out both my dreams, writing and saving the world. My ex-wife always discouraged that." Emory looked off, and a smile appeared in his eyes when he said, "but now there's nothing to hold me back."
~~~~~

Zora was genuinely happy for Emory and his walk of faith. She wondered if Emory felt as if he had gained his freedom or failed his marriage.

Zora found out that Emory and his wife, Olivia, had been married two short years, and no children had come from their union. His wife was a corporate attorney that he had met on a conference and married three months later. In Zora's opinion, Olivia sounded like a snobby woman. She had objected to everything in their marriage from children to his career change. It wasn't until Emory published his first book, *Tears in Africa: Human Rights for the Inhuman?* and it made the *New York Times* best-seller list that Olivia began to take him seriously as a writer. His wife had never supported his idea to go to Africa for research, so legal case studies that he had access to in the states were the basis of his work. Emory expressed that Olivia attempted to navigate his writing in a direction that he didn't wanted it to go. Emory said that she treated his writing like a part-time business, and for him, it had been a full-time passion. He said that Olivia always thought that if he set his goals higher, they could be good together. But he never truly felt that her love for him ran as deep as his for her did.

Zora enjoyed their conversation and could easily relate to Emory's intelligence. Zora had gone to school for seven years to get her doctorate in literature and become a college professor, but she still made a big deal about the extra year that Emory went through to get his JD.

When she announced that she had to get back to the house, she noticed the disappointment on Emory's face, but he extended her an open invite and thanked her for her help.

On the short walk back to her house, she thought of Will and how long they had been keeping company. Then she thought of how in just two hours she knew more about Emory's background than she did about Will's. She made a mental note to mention it the next time she was in his company. When she got inside her house she checked her caller ID, and there was still no Will, but Chelle had called once. She opened up her freezer and took out a pint of ice cream and plopped down on her couch.

She called Chelle back and was appreciative to her for getting her out of the house for a while. Chelle apparently needed a ride to pick up her car, and she did not want to sit around and wait for Will's call all day anyway.

CHELLE

§

"So where you do you want to live when you finish?"

Chelle couldn't stop thinking about the things that Ty had said to her last night. She knew he was drunk, and the next time she saw him he would say that he didn't remember, but her Nana always said that is the best time to hear the truth from someone. She said drinking is like chanting and dancing for some indigenous cultures. It becomes sacred time, and sacred time means being closer to our perceptions of the spiritual worlds. Aunt Mattie was a backwoods roots woman, and if she said that people tell truth when they're drunk, Chelle believed it.

She was trying very hard to concentrate on the conversation that she and her mother, Mai Ling, were having, but thoughts of Ty kept getting in the way.

How could he have been so mean and insensitive? She couldn't get rid of the image of him staggering drunkenly through her door at two in the morning. She'd been waiting. She knew that he'd come there. He thought it was OK to disrespect her in that way and he thought those things because she let him. She had had enough last night, and she had built up the courage to tell him. He must have thought that she would be asleep, because when he flicked on the light and saw her sitting on the couch with her eyes pinned to his, she could read nothing but surprise. She didn't beat around the bush; she just came out with what she wanted to say.

"Hello Tyrone. Where in the hell do you acquire the audacity to creep into my home at this time of morning?" She didn't move from her spot on the couch, but she was pointing her perfectly manicured index finger in his direction while he stood looking at her as if she had lost her ever-lasting mind.

After rolling his red eyes up toward the ceiling, he looked at Chelle and shook his head. "Baby, I just had the type of day that you wouldn't believe. I went over to my moms when I left here and found her passed out on the kitchen floor. I just came from dropping her off back at the house." He paused to make sure that Chelle was taking in the fullness of his lie before continuing. "We were at the hospital all day. The doctor say moms coulda died. She had choked on a fish bone, Chelle." He frowned up his face like he was gonna cry, but went on, "Lord only knows what woulda happened to her if I had not showed up when I did."

Chelle didn't want to call him a straight-up liar for fear that he might be telling the truth, so she just asked, "Ty, why didn't you just call? I would've driven over to the hospital. You should not have had to go through that alone."

He hesitated before speaking, "Well, Vonita came through. Moms really feels deep for her, and I thought it best to leave you out of it. I mean it's nothing personal, but she like fam to moms."

Chelle's mouth dropped in the shape of a small o, "Well then Mr. Vonita, why didn't you roll up in her crib at two in the morning? Why you come up over here if Vonita is such fam?"

She saw anger flash through his eyes, and then it disappeared. "Baby, understand," he began firmly. "Vonita is always gonna be the mother of my kids and plus we got a history. She got a history with my family. Her peeps gone, so all she got is my peeps. I'm cutting for you boo, but you been sheltered and privileged all your life, and I'm beginning to think that you ain't getting it. I been being patient with waiting on you to come around, but this shit just ain't clicking like it should be Chelle."

Chelle stood firm and watched him take her key off his key ring and put it on her coffee table, but when he slammed the front door, she ran out and called to him. How he'd managed to turn the table and have her apologizing between gasps of pleasure was beyond her, but he did.

Chelle was lucky enough to have two parents that loved and cherished each other long before lupus invaded their lives and had money from thriving careers to take care of her until she could take care of herself. She was just as unlucky, because they didn't even live in the state of Texas and most of the time weren't even in the country. Her mother played the viola in an orchestra, and her father was a successful attorney. They met long before Chelle was born when her father was on business in Tokyo, Japan. She had left them in New York when she was only eighteen. Chelle had grown up accustomed to the city life and nannies. She wanted to spend her college years exploring the south and what she thought was important to southerners, family. Her father's sister Aunt Mattie lived in Austin, Texas, and Chelle remembered how she'd always baked and did the things that she longed for her own mother to do when they visited her. Chelle chose to live there near Aunt Mattie. She lived on the campus of the University of Texas at Austin for a whole year before Aunt Mattie took ill. Like Chelle, Aunt Mattie was alone in the world. Her kids were far too successful to suggest more than hiring a nurse to look after their mother. Chelle moved in against her parents' wishes with the aunt that she had grown so close to in the past year to take care of her. School was put on the back burner when her aunt's condition worsened.

Aunt Mattie's diabetes had always caused her to lead a very restrictive diet, but that didn't stop her from cooking up food that Chelle hadn't been raised on. Chelle would laugh when she thought about how she was paper-thin when she first moved to Texas. Her aunt had made sure that she had a piping hot meal at least twice a week. When Aunt Mattie had to get her legs amputated, she and Chelle both took it as a tough blow. Aunt Mattie had been grateful when Chelle moved in with her. She hadn't wanted to live in a nursing home, and she knew that Chelle was making the ultimate sacrifice for her.

Aunt Mattie taught her a lot about life and family during her stay. She was a country woman and had country ways, but that hadn't bothered Chelle. She didn't mind that her Aunt Mattie picked her teeth after dinner with the straw from her broom, or that she believed in going to the roots worker when she felt her sickness taking its toll on her. Chelle didn't eat the pigs' feet or cow tongues that her aunt prepared regularly, but she didn't think any less of Aunt Mattie for eating them either.

Her aunt was beautiful in her eyes. Most people saw the three hundred pounds of flesh that she carried around as her body or the oversized feet that she slid around on shoeless and judged her as someone of lesser value. But Chelle saw beauty. Aunt Mattie's head was shaved completely bald. She made claims that a woman who was in love with her first husband put a Haitian root on her, which caused her hair to fall out and her feet to swell. Chelle thought that the haircut made her look regal and natural. Her scent was cinnamon at all times, and her smile was straight and bright. She had told Chelle in a voice as deep as a large man's, "Had me a man once that knew true beauty. It ain't in size of hips or long curly hair. You reminds me of him. He usta call me Life. I like that now, but then I thought he was crazy. I think he meant that I was real. You get what you get from me. I tell ya Chay, God make somebody out there that's gone love each and every one of us, just like we is. You ain't got ta go round here tryna change fo nobody. Always be who you is, and he'll find you."

She learned a lot about her family and herself from her aunt, and she would always appreciate that. Her father never talked about their family. Seemed he was always too busy chasing his career and Chelle's mother. She found out that Aunt Mattie and her father had left their mother and father, sharecroppers in Mississippi, when Aunt Mattie was just twenty and her father was fourteen. They had never been to Texas, but Aunt Mattie had dreams of becoming an attorney and going to UT Austin. They lived as boarders, and she worked as a maid for five different families. By the time she had enough money saved for her first semester of school, it was time for Chelle's father to start college. So Aunt Mattie gave up her dream and sacrificed her own education for her brother's.

After six months of bonding and caring for each other, Aunt Mattie died. Chelle was devastated. She lied to her parents about going to school for two years before she really went back. She felt that she was right back where she started. Privileged and alone.

When she emerged from her thoughts, her mother was waving her hand in front of her face.

"Yoo whooooo. Rachelle ... Come back to me. I'm talking to you, and you're not even here. I asked you a question."

Her mother was giving her a very annoyed look.

"I'm sorry, mother. I don't know where my mind has been lately. School plus the—"

"No, Rachelle!" Her mother was angry now as she rose from the seat on the breezy patio and threw the napkin that had been in her lap onto the table. Chelle looked around to make sure none of the other restaurant patrons were watching. Her mother was a tiny Asian woman, but her presence demanded too much attention. She had extremely tight eyes, which Chelle had managed to inherit. Chelle had not inherited her silky, straight black hair. Chelle had her father's curly hair, and her mother thought it was beautiful. She was an admirer of the African American race and thought she couldn't have helped make a more perfect child. She focused on her mother's pin-straight, pitch-black hair and her almost white face. When the two women were together, most people didn't identify the small-framed Japanese woman as Chelle's mother. Chelle's skin was much darker and very thick compared to her mother. Chelle's mother was not what one would call a pretty person, but she definitely had a presence that caused people to remember her long after she left a room. Her mother went overboard when it came to trying to assimilate with the black woman's attitude, so in Chelle's eyes, her mother was tripping big time.

"You have been strange ever since dat voodoo Mattie go and die." She was frantically waving her arms and shouting now. Chelle hoped for relief from management, but then she thought about the owner of the upscale seafood steak house. Mai Ling, who usually only came to visit Chelle a couple of times a month, had been here four times in one month. James Jacadi, the ex-professional football player, was the reason for her mother's more frequent visits. He was her new black boy toy, though he was hardly a boy at fifty-eight. Everyone from the head chef to the busboy knew who she was and respected that. There would be no savior at Jacadi's today, because so far Mai Ling had James eating out of the palm of her hand. Her mother was a very married woman—to Chelle's father no less—but sometimes Mai Ling took his sympathy for her disease too far. Her mother's affair was supposed to be a secret, but if Chelle knew about it, she was sure her father did or would know soon, just as he had found out about the her previous two affairs.

"Mother, please. Not here."

Mai Ling looked around at the staring patrons as if she had just become privy that they were in public. She leaned in closer to Chelle, "You know how I felt about that damn woman." Chelle could tell just how angry she was, because her fake ethnic accent was suddenly replaced with her true Japanese one.

Chelle was quiet. She loved Aunt Mattie and was tired of hearing about how much her mother hated her.

"I know she called to her fucking spirits, and they put this disease in my fingers." Her eyes watered as she raised her hands in Chelle's face. She blamed Aunt Mattie for the lupus that had caused her bones to weaken and curve in her fingers. She had always thought she was better than Aunt Mattie and resented the woman because Chelle loved her so much. Aunt Mattie once told Chelle's mother that if she could not be there more often for her daughter because of her cello, then God would move the mountain separating her from her daughter. Her mother had blamed Aunt Mattie for her disease every since.

"She da reason I can't play anymore, and you know it." She grabbed her purse from the edge of the table. "And still after that—even in death, you choose her." She pivoted, twirling on her high stiletto heels and marched out of the restaurant, leaving Chelle alone under the gaze of staring strangers.

DONISHA

§

Marcus had taken Donisha and the kids to the Wax Museum, and now they were on their way to dinner. It had been three weeks since their first date, and she was still impressed by Marcus's style and interest in her children. D'Edward, who went by the name Ed, thought Marcus was the best thing since sliced bread. At eight years old Ed hadn't had much of a father. Big D'Edward had been locked up for two years now for petty drug crimes, but even when he wasn't in jail, he only saw his son about once a year, and he'd lived right around the corner all of Ed's life.

This was only the kids' second meeting with Marcus, but that didn't stop Ed from being excited. Frankie, on the other hand, was a true skeptic. She was only six years old and looked at the man sideways. Donisha knew that Frankie had held a greater bond with her father than Ed had with his own, and she felt that that was the reason for Frankie's skepticism.

"Hey kids," Marcus turned around in the seat of his Cadillac truck as he waited for a stoplight to change. "What do you guys wanna eat?"

"Uh," Ed began, "I want a burger and some fries."

Frankie looked at him, rolled her eyes, and defiantly stated, "I want to eat some of Mommy Nisha's cooking." She looked out the window and turned back toward Marcus and added, "at home."

Marcus looked over at Donisha, unsure of what his next move was supposed to be. He was pleading with his eyes for her to intervene. He felt bad for the little girl. Donisha had told him about the adoption and the difficulty that she was having since her father's death.

"Frankie," Donisha began. After three years she still walked on egg shells with Frankie. She still felt as if she had to try extra hard to gain the love and trust of the little girl that she had so easily given up. "Honey, Minister Black is gonna take us to a restaurant to eat. After we eat, then we can go home. OK?"

Frankie looked at her mother with the same big brown eyes and butter-toned skin as Franko's, and Donisha was sure her heart would melt. This little girl had been taking a piece of her heart every day since she'd come to live with her. This had shocked Donisha, because in the beginning she had wondered if there was room left for anyone else besides Ed. It had become hard for her to imagine a time when she didn't want her. Frankie twirled one of her two curly pigtails before answering her mother. "OK, mommy Nisha."

Donisha wished that there was someway she could get the child to simply call her mama like Ed, but Donisha had been so adamant about her calling her Nisha with Franko. He wouldn't go for his child calling her mother by her first name, so he taught her "mommy Nisha." Here she was sitting in the car with Minister Black and she couldn't stop thinking about all the things that she never said to Franko. She thought about his voice and how stern it was when he spoke to her.

"Donisha, I know how you feel about Frankie even if you don't. I'm sorry if I ruined your little plan to live happily ever after without her, but she is all I got. I want my baby girl to have a family. I want her to have you. I want to have you, but I can't force you into anything." He looked away and Donisha couldn't tell whether he was trying to fight back tears or anger. He turned his face back to her and ran his hand through his coal-black hair.

Even with the situation she felt he had gotten her into, she couldn't help but admire his handsomeness. His skin was a perfectly tanned bronze, and his face was so chiseled that she wanted to touch it and make sure he was real. But it was his eyes that had won her over in the beginning. They could be so big and brown when he was excited or upset, but they held a certain taming tightness when he was calm. She could get lost in his eyes.

"We don't have to be a family Donisha, but she will not call you by your first name. Where I'm from, you don't do that. My mama would roll over in her grave if I let Frankie do that."

Donisha looked at Franko defiantly, "Look man, you brought that child around here all up in my family's life till I didn't have much of a choice to admit that she existed, but I don't have to acknowledge her as my daughter. You stopped that adoption, not me, Franko." She could feel the tears welling up in her eyes as she pointed her finger at his chest. She lowered her voice, so that her father would not come out on the porch, "She's your daughter." Those words had been a stab in the heart for Franko. He had loved that little girl from the moment he laid eyes on her. How could her mother not? His words were soft now, and Donisha had to fight the urge to lean on his chest where she was sure she could find peace. "When she can talk, she will not call you Donisha." He looked off into the night and turned and placed his hand gently on her shoulder. She didn't move, because in all her rebellion she needed his touch. "There will come a time when you won't be proud of the person that you are with her, with me. But I forgive you, Donisha. I love you so much that I'll forgive you for anything. Love forgives." After the words left his lips, he stepped down from the porch steps and walked into the night leaving his statements to penetrate Donisha's mind.

When they turned into the Western Sizzler, Ed went wild. "Yippie, we're going out to eat." He was so excited that Donisha was almost embarrassed. She hadn't taken him out a lot, and it was showing. At least Frankie knew how to conduct herself. She sat staring out the window as if in the backseat of Minister Black's truck was the last place that she wanted to be.

ZORA

§

Zora hadn't seen Will in six days, and he had the nerve to cut their dinner date short because of an emergency at the office. His phone started vibrating like crazy right in the middle of their meal. He said that there was an emergency at the clinic he ran, and while she understood, Zora was still a bit disappointed.

"Baby," he had said in a tone so sexy that she thought she would melt, "These past few months have been incredible with you. Every free minute of my time I've wanted to spend it wrapped inside your legs, but when duty calls, I have to run. I'm trying to build something here, a name for myself and a future for us." He cupped her small hand inside his own and kissed it softly. "I promise I'll be back as soon as I'm done. If not, I'll be here first thing in the morning, because we have a date at church, remember?" His words were like music to Zora's ears. This man wanted to make a life with her. As much effort as he put into his work, he had to have been the best damned doctor around.

As she got out of his Benz and closed the door, she sighed, "I guess this is what I get for wanting a professional man." She chuckled as she opened up her bag to fish for her keys. Will drove off before she made it to her porch, but she shrugged it off as him being in a rush. Just as she pulled her keys out, she saw Emory jogging up the other side of the street, sweat streaming down his face.

"Late night jog?" she called out to him. He spotted her and treaded over.

"Only way to do it," he replied happily. Emory was now standing in front of her panting lightly.

Zora chuckled and offered him a drink inside.

"So, Zora," he began after she handed him the cold glass of water. "Where is the best place to fellowship with other Christian folk around here?" His voice was light and congenial.

Zora had failed to notice a few things about Emory during their last encounter. He was very nice looking. The tank shirt that he was wearing accented every cut that his well-worked-out body held, and he seemed a lot taller tonight. He was definitely taller than Will. And the man had dimples so deep that she could see them when he talked.

"Excuse me? I didn't catch that Emory." She had been so busy staring at him that she had not heard a word he'd said.

"Church," he stated with a lighthearted laugh, "I was looking for a good church to visit tomorrow."

"Oh, that's easy. You can visit Victory and Praise with me if you want. It's Baptist, but it's a good church." She walked over and sat on the love seat across from Emory. "So were you brought up in the church?"

Emory's eyebrows went up as if he was surprised by her response to his question as well as her question to him.

"Hmmmm. That's a hard one. See my mama used to make me go, but I never listened to anything the pastor or ministers said once I got there. I don't even think I really believed in God." He looked down at his hands. "When I was in high school, I was responsible for getting one of my classmates pregnant. She wanted an abortion, and I don't know why, but I talked her into keeping the baby. I guess deep down inside I had an opinion about abortion that I really felt I had no right to voice as a male. Anyway, we had a beautiful daughter. We named her Faith. She had the chubbiest cheeks and the tightest eyes that you ever did see." He paused and looked over at Zora. "Faith is who and what changed my life. I was such a slacker until her. My folks were disappointed in me long before Faith happened. I mean, I come from a family where I didn't have to work for anything. So I did what I wanted. I slept around, smoked pot, and broke as many laws as I possibly could. Then God sent me my sweet-eyed angel." He dropped his head for a moment, and when he looked up at Zora, his eyes were glazed over. He wasn't crying, but Zora sensed a deep sadness there. "When she was a year old, she woke up one day not feeling well. Not that she could talk or anything, but you know how babies communicate? Whining and tears." A look of remembrance fell over his face and he chuckled.

"We thought it was her teething, so we took her to her pediatrician and he confirmed just that. But the next day she was gone. Autopsy report called it myocarditis, an inflammation of the heart. I had to start believing in something to deal with that. I chose God."

"I'm so sor—," Zora began.

"No, Zora. Don't be sorry, because I'm not. God knows just what to do to get us to look at him."

They sat in the uncomfortable silence for about twenty seconds before Zora spoke. "Well, Emory, you're welcome to visit the church that I fellowship with anytime."

Emory stood and looked over at Zora, offering her a very sexy smile. "You know what, Zora? I may have to take you up on that offer."

By the time Emory got to Zora's front door, she had given him the directions and the start time of service. Zora didn't claim to be sold out to Christ, but she did like to go to church and she did love the Lord, so she was happy to be able to help Emory find a place to worship for the time being. After she let him out, she thought about his daughter and how hard that must have been. She had dealt with loss, a similar loss. She knew the pain he must have felt.

Zora dressed slowly for church the next morning. She was waiting on Will's call. When Zora hadn't heard from him by ten, she was pretty sure that he wasn't going to come to church with her. She called his cell phone and left a message giving him the address and headed out her front door. Donisha had called and informed her that she didn't need a ride this Sunday, so Zora planned to head straight for the church. As she drove past Emory's house, she saw him walking down his walkway adjusting his tie. She pulled up to the curb and took a mental note of how good he looked in his Hugo Boss slacks and his crisp white shirt. She rolled down the window and honked her horn to get his attention.

"Good morning," he waved as he spotted her, "How are you today?"

She opened the door and stepped out of her car as Emory approached. "I'm good. I was on my way to the church, and I wanted to make sure that the directions I gave you were sufficient enough for you to find your way this morning."

"You look good this morning, that's for sure. And the directions you gave me are fine; although as you can see, I haven't had a chance to use them. If you don't mind, I would like for you to ride along with me so there is no chance of me being late." He looked over at her face and noticed the hesitation in her eyes. "I'm sorry. I understand that you may have plans before or after the services. Would it be OK if I just followed you?"

"No," Zora began. "It's fine. I don't mind riding with you. I don't have plans at all. I have a few friends that attend Victory and Praise that can get me home if that's not a problem." The only friend Zora was concerned with riding home with was Will. Riding to church with Emory was actually a good idea. That way after church Will would have to spend time with her because she wouldn't have a ride home. She smiled at her own wit as Emory closed the passenger side door to his Tahoe after making sure that she was comfortably seated.

Zora couldn't believe that she and Emory had been able to find seats next to Donisha, her kids, and Chelle in the crowded church.

Pastor Leo was an elderly man and, in Zora's opinion, quite the colorful character. His sermon seemed to be eloquent, but Zora couldn't really get into it. What she did manage to do throughout the service was silently pray to God for Will to walk through the door.

After Donisha noticed Zora's rubber neck halfway through the service, she nudged her in the side with her elbow. "What are you lookin fo, Zo?"

Zora was unaware that she was being watched, and embarrassment engulfed her.

She leaned in to whisper back to Donisha, "What chu talking about? Nothin', girl. I'm not looking for a thing." Donisha gave her a "yeah right" look.

Zora was glad when she realized the service was about to end. She hadn't been into it and decided that the message just hadn't been for her. Jamie signaled the end of the service. She always did with her Holy Ghost dance. She was practically as quiet as a church house mouse until the end of service when Pastor Leo would do what the women called the "rise-and-fall altar call."

So every Sunday right at altar call, Jamie started bouncing around the front of the church and waving her arms like she was on fire.

Zora didn't see Will after the service and was disappointed that he couldn't make more room for her—even more so, she was disappointed by the idea that he couldn't make room for God at all in his busy life.

After the service they all met outside with the other church members. She introduced Emory to Chelle and Donisha. As the four of them stood chatting about Emory's old home, Kyla approached them with her patient, Peter, close in tow.

"Hello people," she chimed in, "How is everybody? I see we have a new addition to our clique, and if I might add, he is a mighty fine one."

They exchanged greetings and hugs. Zora introduced Emory to Kyla and Peter.

"So, anybody want to go to BeeBee's for Sunday dinner?" Zora offered. She was hungry and bored and could not see herself going home right away after the way Will had stood her up.

"Uh," Chelle started, "I have plans. Sorry, Zoe, but I'm out today."

"Me too girl," Donisha stated matter-of-factly, "Marcus—I mean Minister Black—is taking me and the kids to meet his mother today." She looked over at her daughter and shrugged after she was unable to read the blank expression on the child's face.

Zora looked at Kyla but felt let down when Kyla stated, "Girl, Peter and I are driving up to San Antonio as soon as we leave here. He's never been to the Riverwalk or Sea World. We gon' have a ball!" Kyla giggled, and Peter offered Zora an apologetic smile and added, "Sorry Zoe, maybe next time." Zora nodded at Peter. Peter was a fairly handsome bleached blond, perfectly tanned white guy. He wore his hair in the spike style that a lot of the white guys looked good with. He was always dressed rugged casual, but his style became him. Zora hadn't thought it was possible to be ruggedly neat until she met Peter, but there he was standing in all his rugged neatness. Peter wore a camel-colored suit with a deep chocolate shirt underneath. Zora had never been into white boys, especially white boys with HIV, but Peter was extremely easy on the eyes.

Zora was almost hypnotized by his deep blue eyes until she heard Emory's voice.

"I guess I'm the only one free today, neighbor." Emory had an unsure smile plastered across his face, and Zora felt sorry for him. She smiled in his direction and answered, "Well your company is good enough for me."

Emory and Zora decided that they would eat at Red Lobster, because Emory had a taste for their famous bread. Zora was amazed at how comfortable she felt around Emory. He was humble and attentive, and he never once tried to come on to her.

"So Mr. Hernes," Zora stated jokingly after she had placed her order for stuffed shrimp and Emory had ordered his lobster, "how are things going in the new house?"

Emory smiled at Zora before answering and looked as if he wanted to say something other than what came from his mouth. "Well, everything seems to be going perfect. I received a call from one of my missionary friends, and he seems to think that I could be of use in Africa right now. Ethiopia to be exact." He chuckled before continuing, "At first he was calling to see if I could give him any information on how political asylum is granted in the United States. He wanted to know if I wanted to help because of my experience with law. I was still practicing in the employment sector the last time we spoke."

He paused and a half smile slid across his lip. "He didn't even know that I had left."

He looked into Zora's eyes and for a second she truly believed that he was looking inside her. "People have been dying of AIDS for decades while I've been sipping Merlot and enjoying fine dining. I told Roy that I want to be there with them, and he was thrilled."

"So you're going to Africa?" Zora asked in amazement.

"Yep, I leave on August 15th. I'm so excited. This trip has been my dream for as long as I can remember."

His smile was so wide that Zora was sure that the sun slept somewhere in his throat.

"I have never been anywhere that wasn't on vacation. My friend runs a camp there for refugees. I'll be helping to transport food, medical supplies, and probably a bit of legal advice. Although I don't feel that legal advice will mean a lot to people who are starving or suffering from AIDS in a war torn country, Roy says that it could help rescue some to safety.

"He warned me of the danger, but to me the only danger is sitting by and letting those that cannot help themselves die."

They both sat in silence as their friendly waiter dispersed their meals. After they let him know that they were satisfied with their food, he walked away with promises of returning to check on them later.

For a reason that was unclear at the time, but she would later call fate, Zora turned her head in the direction of the entrance and what she saw nearly made her choke on the piece of shrimp that she was chewing. How did he know that she was here and what would he say about her being here with Emory? She looked over at Emory who had a strange and worried look on his face. "Are you OK, Zora?" His voice was full of concern, and he appeared to be getting up from his seat to come to her aid. She nodded her head and waved her hand at him as a gesture to stay seated. She struggled to keep her composure as she caught her breath, thinking of a way to go over to Will and let him know that she had waited and he never called. She had to let him know that Emory was just a friend, and she had no romantic interest in him. She did not want him to get the wrong idea and think she was actually there on a date with Emory.

After a few minutes and a couple sips of water, Zora's breathing returned to normal. Emory, who had seemed uneasy in his inability to ease her breathing asked her again, "Are you sure you're OK, Zora?"

Zora nodded and let out a high-pitched, fake laugh, "I'm fine Em. We all get a little choked up sometimes."

Emory smiled and tilted his head, "My mom used to call me that."

The thought of being spotted with a strange man before she had a chance to explain the situation to Will made Zora nervous, and although she didn't want to be blatantly rude, she had to get over there.

She began to shift in her seat, and Emory's smile disappeared, "Is something wrong, Zora?"

"Yes," she replied, "Would you excuse me? I have to go to the bathroom. My little choking fit kind of threw off my balance."

"Sure," he answered, "Go ahead. I'll be right here when you get back."

Since Will didn't see Zora when he came in, she almost had to chase him to where he was being seated. She stopped mid-stride when she saw the woman and little boy waiting for him at the table. She watched as he kissed the woman on the cheek and rubbed the top of the little boy's head. She felt a burning sensation in her eyes but knew that there was some sort of explanation for this. She wished that the woman was a cousin or sister visiting and that would make the situation OK. That would explain why he'd stood her up at church, but she knew better. She knew the woman had to be his lover. It pissed her off to no end too. He had stood her up. She had to let him know that she saw him, and she had to let the woman know that she'd been with him.

She walked over to where he had sat down, and he looked up at her with startled eyes that screamed, "Please don't!"

"Hello Will," she began, "I saw you come in, and since you are such a hard person to get a hold of, I decided to come over and let you know that I waited all morning for you sweetie." She gently placed her hand on his cheek, and he swatted it away.

The woman sat there dumbfounded while Zora took in her appearance. She was a big girl, and if she was a love interest of Will's, then he had bad taste. Her complexion was dark, blue-black almost, but that wasn't what made her ugly. In fact Zora had always pondered having skin as smooth and dark as the beautiful Sudanese model Alek Wek. This woman's skin, however, was full of craters and bumps that appeared to have tiny people living inside of them. She looked as if she had lotioned her face and hands with cooking oil, and her teeth were so big that they hung out of her mouth while it was closed. Wearing a slightly askew, too large blond wig, her appearance screamed loud enough to get far more attention than this boogawolf needed. Zora decided that the woman looked like a gorilla in a wig.

Zora looked at the woman and stuck out her hand while saying, "I'm sorry. Will is so rude. I'm Zora, Will's friend." She looked over at Will, who looked as if he was about to crap his pants. "His close friend," she added. The wigged gorilla left Zora's hand hanging and looked over at Will.

"Will, don't you lie, niggah. Ima ask you one time and you needs to come correct."

Will seemed horrified. He looked back up at Zora with pleading eyes. He found no sympathy there, so he turned to face the wigged gorilla seated at the table with him.

"Who is this woman?" Zora almost cracked up laughing at how loud the wigged gorilla began to bark at Will in public.

Will looked as if he was about to cry, but he didn't open his mouth. Zora looked over at the little boy and it could not be mistaken that he was Will's son. He was the spitting image of Will. Even with his mother's color, he had the same foreign look as his father. The gorilla held up her hand and showed Zora her ring. "Well Zora, Will ain't supposed to have no female friends that I don't know nothing about, but since he playing stupid, won't you tell me about ya'll friendship?"

It was amazing that they had managed to not make a scene at that point, but after Zora told Will's wife about how they met and the things they had done, it was on. The wigged gorilla started cussing and screaming at Will and finally ended up knocking him out of his chair. The wigged gorilla finally stopped hitting him long enough to start crying and grab her son's hand and make her way to the door. Zora saw Emory standing in the crowd watching and held her finger up for him to wait as she ran behind her. She felt bad, and she had to let the woman know that she didn't mean to be a part of anything done to hurt her.

"What?" the woman spat when Zora finally caught up with her at Will's Mercedes.

"I didn't know about you," Zora was stuttering and she really did feel bad for this woman, "He didn't tell me he was married. I would have never called him had I known." She didn't expect a response from the weeping woman.

"For all it's worth, ma'am, I'm sorry." Zora had tears streaming down her face now too, but she knew that it had nothing to do with the other woman's pain.

The woman's face softened, and Zora could see pain in her eyes, "I know girl, I don't even blame you." She put her head down and started playing with her keys, "I bet he told you he was a doctor, didn't he?"

Zora's eyes widened, "He is, isn't he?" She knew the truth before the question escaped her lips.

"He tells em all that. Will ain't got a dime. I bought him his car, and he spends my money. My mama died six years ago in a hit-and-run accident by a diesel. My family settled out of court for six million dollars." Zora watched as a smile formed through the woman's tears. "Four years ago when Tavion was first born, Will wasn't like this. But shoot," she sighed and looked down at herself, "I wasn't like this. I was small like you, and I could keep my man. My money keeps him now, but I want it to be me again." When she lifted her eyes to Zora again, all softness had disappeared. "I been in Louisiana for three months cause my sister was sick, but I'm back now. I appreciate you coming out and letting me know your part." She looked down at her hands thoughtfully before looking back at Zora.

"But I love him and regardless of what he do, Ima keep him. So now that you know about me, please respect me and don't call my house or my man."

Zora nodded her head at the woman as she pulled out of the parking space. She had a newfound respect for the pain of an ugly woman. She turned to walk into the restaurant just in time to see Emory walking toward her.

CHELLE

§

She had felt bad for lying to Zora, but ever since the day that Ty had accidentally switched their phones, she had been receiving all kinds of crazy messages on her voice mail. He never even knew that he didn't have his own phone, so Chelle guessed that he went on making calls as usual. Chelle had traded phones back without even alerting Ty to the fact that there had been a mix-up in the first place. But Ty still had incoming calls on Chelle's phone.

The weirdest message had come through the night before, and she had planned on doing her own investigating to find out what the message meant. She thought about the whiny voiced girl on her voice mail and knew it wasn't Vonita.

"Hey Ty, it's me," the voice began. This was the fourth time that Chelle had listened to it and she couldn't help but wonder where she knew the voice from.

"You said that you was gonna have that money I needed. You know I got business to take care of, and if I don't get this done soon, it will be too late. I don't know who else to call or where else to go without getting you in trouble. You said if someone finds out, momma will kill me. I don't have nowhere to go. I'm scared. Please help me."

The message hurt Chelle, because Ty had asked her for four hundred dollars on Saturday morning. She had told him that she could give it to him that night, but he never came back to her house. She wanted to kick herself for all the times that she had given him money in the past. Had he been giving her money to other women all along?

She sat on her couch contemplating her next move and calling herself stupid for getting involved with such a loser in the first place. Her cell phone rang, and she looked at the unfamiliar number and let it go to voice mail. Chelle had never liked the sound of her own voice on recording systems, so her voice mail greeting was still the default message that came with the phone. Whoever was calling had no idea that they were getting Chelle's phone, so the caller didn't hesitate to leave a message for Ty.

The alert that let her know she had a new voice mail chirped in her ear, and she called her voice mail box to listen.

"Hey, it's me again. I was just calling to give you the address so that you could meet me up there on Monday. And the lady that answered the phone said that since I'm only fourteen, an adult is gonna have to sign for me. I just told her that my father was bringing me, so you gon have to act like you my daddy." She rattled off the address in a shaky voice and ended her call with, "Please be there Ty. I didn't ask for this."

Chelle sat there in shock. What business would Ty possibly have to take care of with that baby? Chelle decided right then and there that she wouldn't tell Ty about the message, but she would show up there herself. She wanted to know what was going on with him, and she was gonna find out.

DONISHA

§

"Oh Marcus, she is pretty and those kids are the most darling things you'd ever want to see," Donisha smiled as Mrs. Black complimented her to Marcus. "That little girl looks like she mixed with something with all that pretty hair." She looked at Donisha and sighed.

"Excuse me baby if I'm embarrassing you, but you the first woman that my son has ever brought home. I been waiting on this day for thirty years."

"Ma," Marcus began with a chuckled rustling in his throat, "Stop or you'll make her so uncomfortable that she'll never come back," Marcus looked over at Donisha and winked.

"OK, I'll stop, because this is definitely a woman I'd like to become a regular guest in my home." She smiled and stopped stirring her greens long enough to kiss her son on the cheek.

Marcus grabbed Donisha's hand and led her out to the front porch where they sat on an old porch swing. Donisha was amazed at how well her children had taken to Marcus's parents. Frankie had become putty in his father's hands the moment he spoke to her. Donisha figured it was because he reminded her of her late grandfather whom she loved almost as much as Franko. They hadn't even looked up from the game of chess that he was trying to teach them when Marcus had led her outside.

Marcus's parents had a nice size house away from the bustle of the city. It was like one of those country farms that she had seen on television. All of the windows had shutters and a big tractor sat out back in front of a barn. Marcus said that they had chickens in a chicken coop further back on the land, and Donisha and the kids had seen horses and cows grazing the pasture as soon as they arrived.

"I can't believe this is so calming Marcus." She had just recently become used to calling him by his first name, and it still felt weird escaping her lips. "Being here with you and being able to—" she paused and looked at him. His eyes encouraged her to continue. "I'm just not used to being me. Ya know? Letting my true feelings show. My daddy used to say that every man was gonna pay for what Ed's daddy did to me. But I don't want to make anyone else suffer because I told the wrong guy I loved him."

Marcus put his hand under her chin and lifted her face so that she could see his eyes and the sincerity they held. "Donisha, your father was the wisest of them all, and the rest of us can only be honored to follow in his footsteps. I wouldn't want to do anything to hurt his daughter."

He bent into her face and kissed her softly. When he pulled away from her, there were tears in her eyes. "I know that you are wounded, Donisha. I don't know what you have been through, but I wanna be here for you, and with the help of God we can get through this."

Until that moment, Donisha hadn't been able to take her relationship with Marcus seriously. She had only been after God, because she was after her father and she knew that because of his life, he was definitely with God. She had originally thought that Marcus was her link to God, but the past few months with him had been life transforming for her. She didn't know if it was because of Marcus or because she really wanted to please her father or God, but she was feeling something different from anything she had ever felt before. She had been so much more attentive to her children, and she had even actually listened to the sermon at church today instead of running off at the mouth. She didn't even feel comfortable about dancing at Brown Sugar anymore. Marcus still didn't know that she humped poles to make sure her children were properly clothed and fed. He thought she was a barmaid at the club and that was the reason why they had to leave his parents' house so early. Donisha had missed a lot of money hanging out with Marcus the past few weeks, and it was getting close to time for the kids to go back to school from summer vacation. She had serious shopping to do, and she needed to make the money to do it with. But she had surprised herself when she knelt to pray before bed one night and asked God to make way for her to get the money to provide for her children by dancing for it.

"Marcus, you are a good man and any fool of a woman can see that. I don't have low self-esteem or anything, but what do you want with me? I have baggage so extreme that any man in his right mind would run the other way from me. I have seen the streets from top to bottom, and believe me, you don't know or want to know the half of what I mean by that."

Marcus chuckled and smiled at some far place before replying in a low voice, "I'm not your average man; I am not your average man. We all fall short. No one is perfect, Donisha."

Donisha was grateful for the soft kiss that he leaned in to give her after those words, but she was even more grateful when he didn't ask what she meant by her previous remark.

That night when she dropped the kids off at her mother's before she went to work, she sat in her mother's car and thought about Franko. She wished that she knew the things about life then that she knew now. She would have said yes to him when he asked her to be his wife. She had done everything in her power to break that man and he'd still loved her. She remembered the last conversation that she had with him three years ago.

"Donisha, I love you so much. I love Ed like he's my own and Lord knows that I'd give Frankie the moon." He paused to see her reaction to his declaration. It had been four years since Frankie's birth, and although she had dated and slept around with a large number of guys since Franko, he was the only one that she carried true feeling for. She would never tell him that though. It would be going against everything that she felt was right. She wasn't ready to forgive him for stopping the adoption and bringing that unwanted child into her life. She wanted to make him suffer by wanting but not having something that she could only give him. Her. She knew that his love for her ran deep, but she had been so degraded and abused by other men that she didn't see the worth in herself that he did. He was the only person that had called her up that night with plans to celebrate her birthday.

"Well Franko, you probably shoulda thought about the fact that you was gon want a mother for your child before you decided to go be the cape crusader and play daddy." Her remark hurt him, but he kept pouring his soul out to her. Franko had made a lot of changes in his life for Frankie. Unlike Donisha, he finished school and got a job as a police officer. He said it wasn't his dream career move, but it offered good health insurance and kept a roof over his daughter's head.

He slid his hand over hers and she thought her heart would melt. After all that she had gone through with Franko, his touch still did that to her. When he moved his hand, a small but elegant diamond ring sat on the back of her hand. His eyes smiled at her as he mouthed, "Will you?" It took everything in her to keep her cool and slid the ring over to him, shaking her head no. She wanted to say yes, but she was not ready to stop punishing him.

With defeat in his eyes he spoke, "I'm sorry for anything that I've ever done to hurt you, and I want you to know that I will always love you. When you look on these times with regret and you wonder if I'm mad or grudging, I'm not. I love you and love forgives."

Two weeks later, little Frankie had to come live with Donisha and Ed in their new apartment that the housing authority had granted them with. Franko had been killed in the line of duty. He pulled over some wacko for a routine traffic stop, and the guy shot him. The guy thought that Franko was going to search the car and find the dime bag of weed that was under the driver's seat.

Even though Franko left insurance policies that would take care of Frankie, Donisha cried. She cried because she knew that she could never love Frankie the way Franko had, but most of all she cried because she never once told Franko she loved him.

Before starting the car, she looked toward the sky and for the first time since she got pregnant with Frankie, she really talked to Franko.

"Franko, I'm sorry," she tried wiping the tears away, but they were coming too fast. "I loved you more than you knew. I wanted to be with you more than you knew. I was so stupid, Franko, and now you're gone. Please forgive me. If you can hear me, baby please forgive me."

She thought she was crazy when she heard the wind whisper, "Love forgives."

ZORA

§

As Zora dressed for work the Monday following her episode with Will and the wigged gorilla at Red Lobster, she couldn't rid her mind of what Emory had said to her afterwards. She had told him the whole story once they were in his truck but had regretted asking for his opinion about her situation.

"I'm not saying that you shouldn't have been hurt Zora, but your actions in that restaurant were only centered around your feelings. You didn't think about Will, his wife, or his kid. You didn't even allow yourself room enough to be courteous to me." He looked over at her as he turned on their street. "I'm not trying to offend you Zora, but maybe you should start to consider others in your decisions."

Zora could see that Emory really wasn't trying to offend her, but his brashness had pissed her off. Who did he really think he was to talk to her that way? She looked at him in disbelief.

"Look Emory, I see what you are trying to get at, and I don't have a selfish bone in my body. I wasn't going over there to make trouble for Will and his family. Those were his skeletons that fell out of his closet. You don't even know what the hell is going on between Will and me." She opened the car door, and Emory put his hand on her shoulder.

"Zora, I'm not trying to judge you, and if that's what I sound like, I'm sorry." He put his head down. "I just see so much in you, and I thought that you would understand where I'm coming from. You aren't selfish Zora. You care so much about others. I just thought that maybe I could help you see that." Zora looked Emory dead in his eyes before replying. She could see his sincerity, but she didn't care. He needed to be put in his place.

"Whatever, Emory." was all she said before climbing out of his truck.

When Zora walked out into the morning heat, she cringed at the thought of how the mid-day temperature would be. It was the second week of June, and she knew it would only get hotter. She was glad that she had chosen the thin, white linen pants and sleeveless red Gap logo tee to wear for the day. Since this was summer school, she could be comfortable, and she knew that she wouldn't get too hot during the long walk from her car to the college. She looked down the street toward Emory's house and saw him watering his lawn. Before she could turn her head away from him, he threw up his hand to wave. Zora didn't smile or wave at her neighbor's friendly gesture. She let Emory know that she saw him with the long stare she gave before turning to her car.

It was only after she sat down in the driver seat that she noticed the folded piece of paper underneath her windshield wiper. She got out and lifted the wiper to get the piece of paper. She stood beside the car while she opened the paper and began reading the letter addressed to her.

ZORA

§

I apologize for yesterday. In my past profession there was an advantage to being outspoken, but I guess in friendships that quality is not a good thing. This friendship thing is new to me, so I will probably make a few mistakes at first. Zora, this is my plea to you. Right now I could use a friend and from what happened yesterday I'm sure you could too. I would like for us to start over if that's OK with you. You are a beautiful person, and I am truly sorry if I made you feel anything other than that.

With high hopes,
Emory

Zora looked up from the letter to see if he was still outside, but Emory was gone. She was touched by his efforts, but she had to get to class. If she was more than ten minutes late, she would find her lecture hall deserted.

CHELLE

§

Chelle was nervous as she sat in the parking lot of Planned Parenthood. She had found the address easy since the salon where she got her hair done was in the same shopping center. She didn't know how the girl looked or what to expect from the child, but she was looking for a little girl either being dropped off or on the bus.

At 7:54 a car pulled up and dropped off a woman that looked to be about twenty. Two minutes later a girl walked by Chelle's car and walked up toward the building. She put her hand on the door handle and looked around before going inside. Chelle knew that was her. She didn't look fourteen. In fact, she had a grown woman's body. She was petite, but had curves in all the places that they were supposed to be. The only way that you could tell she was young was by the way she wore her hair. She wore one ponytail that sat on top of her head and sprouted what looked like a fan at the end. She had a backpack on, and Chelle knew that she was supposed to be in school.

Chelle got out of her car and pushed the remote on her key ring to lock it. When she got to the door that the girl had disappeared through, she paused. She looked down at herself to make sure that she blended in well with the environment. She had decided not to put on the regular Ellen Tracy suits that she wore when going to school; she dressed down in a pair of Levi's, a T-shirt, and some tennis shoes. By the time she made it to the waiting area of the clinic, the girl had already signed in and was reading a magazine.

Chelle went and sat beside the girl and for a moment believed that she had lost her nerve. Before she realized that the words came out of her mouth, she heard them.

"Ty's not coming." The girl looked at her with a surprised expression that said she needed an explanation. The girl reached down and put her hand on her backpack, and Chelle began to speak again.

"It was my phone that you left the message on." She had concern in her voice when she asked the girl, "Why do you need Ty to meet you here?"

The child stood up with watery eyes and walked toward the exit. Chelle jumped up and followed her. Once they were outside, she could hear the little girl sobbing. Chelle walked over to her and put her hand on her shoulder. The girl turned and collapsed inside Chelle's arms.

Chelle guided the girl to her car and opened the passenger door for her. The girl sat down and waited for Chelle to get in on her side. Once Chelle was in and the car was started, the girl began to talk.

"I didn't know who you was cause you ain't as big as Ty made you out to be." She looked at Chelle and then looked away. "You're pretty too. He didn't tell me that." She kept looking out the window as Chelle pulled out of the parking space. "Ty is my mama's, boyfriend's brother. That's how I know him." She started sobbing again, "I didn't mean for this to happen. They left us at the house and he touched me on my leg and I just don't know what happened." She was crying out loud now.

Chelle kept driving until she came to a small deli. She parked and looked over at the child in her car.

"What's your name sweetie?"

With her face still toward the window, the girl answered, "Mia."

Chelle stuck out her hand for Mia to shake and to her surprise she took it.

"Well Mia, I'm Chelle. Let's go in here and have us a little lunch."

Mia smiled through her tears and reached for the door handle.

Chelle was overwhelmed with emotion by the time she dropped Mia off in the same projects that Donisha lived in. Whatever feelings she had for Ty had dissolved during her conversation with the young girl. Mia told her how Ty had taken her virginity one day when her mother and his brother were gone. He had been having sex with the child on a regular basis every since then. She had felt hot tears burn her eyes when the girl told her, "He said if I let him stick his thing in me, he would be my boyfriend and buy me stuff. He said if I didn't he would do it anyway, and I wouldn't get nothing."

Mia's mother and Ty's brother were addicted to crack, and Ty knew that most of the time the child was home alone, so he went there and had her whenever he wanted. Chelle was shocked to find out that Ty was so perverted and sick.

Mia had found out that she was pregnant a month ago, and Ty had promised her that he would pay for an abortion with Chelle's money. Mia was young and afraid. Chelle gave Mia her phone number and address and told the child that she shouldn't be so hard on herself. She assured the girl that it was not her fault that a grown man took advantage of her naiveté; she told Mia that Ty was the adult in the situation and he should be held responsible, but Mia made her promise not to tell anyone. She said that Ty supplied her mother with most of her drugs, and she would be in the doghouse more than she already was if he got into any type of trouble. Mia's mother already neglected her for drugs. She did everything short of selling the child's body to feed her habit, and Mia found that it was better to blend in with the filthy walls at home than to make her presence known by telling her mother about Ty's abuse from the very beginning.

It was after five when she pulled her car into her parking spot in front of her apartment. She didn't notice Ty's Regal parked in the visitor's space until she had closed her car door. She silently prepared herself to throw Ty out of her house and out of her life.

She walked into the quiet apartment, and Ty came out of the kitchen.

"Baby," he stated while open his arms for a hug. Chelle backed away from his embrace and looked up at him. An uneasy feeling came over her, and she began to fidget. She had no idea why she was suddenly afraid of Ty, or maybe she did. She wasn't afraid of him before, because she hadn't known that he was a rapist. And even though Mia was a helpless child in Chelle's eyes, a rapist was a rapist.

"Uh, h-hey," she managed to stutter, "I didn't expect to find you here."

He eyed her suspiciously. Chelle had never pulled away from him. "Well baby, can't ya man miss you and wonta see ya?"

Feeling a sudden eruption of bravery in the pit of her stomach, Chelle looked him straight in the eye and said, "I'm glad you're here. I think we need to talk."

After she led him in the house, the soft look on his face disappeared.

"Awh hell, here we fuckin' go! Damn Chelle, I wish like hell you'd stop riding me so hard about Von. I'm here with you and—"

"This is not about Vonita, Ty," she caught him off guard with a deep yell that caused his eyes to buck. He was used to the high-pitched winy nature of her pleas. The extreme control she exhibited shocked him.

"WHAT THEN, CHELLE? WHAT THE FUCK IS IT THEN!?" His voice boomed, which caused Chelle to step further away from. She knew that he thought he had successfully calmed her down, but he was wrong. He had only managed to piss her off even more. Here he was a pedophile screaming at her like he had a right to.

She eyed him defiantly, "We don't really know each other."

A grinch-like smirk spread across his face, "Awh, baby come here." He thought he had won like all the other times. He had not read her boldness; he only saw defeat.

"I know everything I need to know about you, suga." He moved toward her with hunger in his eyes.

She held up her hands and blurted out, "Look Ty, I don't think this is gonna work. I can't play these games with you anymore an—."

He stopped mid-step in his effort to embrace her, "What are you talking about Chelle?" he yelled, "Damn, this shit is why I stay away. Every time I'm in this piece, you bitching. Maybe if you shut the fuck up sometime somebody'll want to fool wit you."

Chelle looked at him in disbelief, "Ty I know about Mia and I—,"

Before she could finish her sentence, he was on her like a wild dog. He slapped her across the face and when she went to swing back, he grabbed her by the neck. She was gasping for air as he screamed and cursed at her.

"Bitch, you don't know shit. I'll kill yo ass. I ain't going down behind no young ass ho that can't keep her legs closed. All you had to do was gimmie the money."

He had her leaning backwards against her dining room table. Chelle reached for the vase that sat in the center of the table. Ty was so busy trying to squeeze the life from her body that he didn't even notice that she almost had her hands on a defense weapon. When she had a good grip on it, she picked it up and hit Ty over the head with it. He stumbled back and touched his head which was now bloody with pieces of what used to be her vase stuck in it. At the sight of the blood on his hands, he turned to Chelle with evil eyes.

"That was the wrong move, bitch!" Chelle staggered over to the living area, tripping over her own legs. Ty was mad, and she knew that he could really hurt her if he caught her. She had to get to Lucy, the duct-tape wrapped bat that Ty had brought over for protection weeks ago. He had no idea that the bat was under the couch. She had put it there when she learned that Vonita knew where she lived.

She was almost there when she felt his fist smash into the back of her head. The blow took her down. She could only muster up enough strength through her daze to turn over on her back. Ty crawled his way up her body placing all of his weight on top of her.

"You know about Mia, huh?" He whispered with something between love and evil in his throat. Ty put his hand on Chelle's face and began squeezing her cheeks between his forefinger and his thumb.

"I'll show you what you know." He started pulling at her clothes with his free hand. Ty had her trapped between the coffee table and the couch. Chelle stretched her arm and managed to grip the end of the bat. At that moment, she began to squirm under Ty.

"Don't fight it, baby. You know this what you want. Daddy always make it better wit dis."

She gathered her strength and swung the bat, but only knocked him off of her. While he was trying to figure out where the blow came from, she regained her composure and swung again. This time the bat met with his skull. He fell out cold on top of her. She lay there with a throbbing face until she felt she had regained the strength to push him off of her. She ran into the kitchen, picked up her cordless phone, and dialed 911. She didn't have time to speak with the cops, because she didn't know when Ty would come to, so she just laid the phone on the couch and ran over to where his limp body was sprawled beside her dining room table.

She kicked his body to make sure that he wasn't playing possum and waiting to attack her when she was close enough to him. He groaned and moved his head to the side in response to her kick and that satisfied her. She began to unlace the brand-new Nikes that he was wearing—the brand-new Nikes that she bought. When she was done, she used one string to tie his hands together as tight as she could. She used the other string to tie his feet together. Then she sat and waited. The cops were on their way, and Ty was gonna pay for what he'd done to her.

As she sat next to his still body, she decided that he was going to pay for what he'd done to Mia too.

After the police took Ty away, Chelle began to feel guilty about her broken promise to Mia. She had told the police everything. She had even let them listen to the messages from Mia that she had saved on her voice mail. A forensic detective had come out and taken pictures of her face and neck. Chelle's face was swollen where Ty had slapped her and her neck was purple from where he had choked her so hard. That day didn't happen to be Ty's lucky day. When they cops searched him they had found three small vials of crack in his sock, which triggered a search of his vehicle. They found a bag containing 150 ecstasy pills and a gun that had been used to rob and kill a drug lord a month ago.

When Ty did come to, he was so mad that his eyes turned red. After they found his drugs and the gun, he must have lost it, because he started cussing and screaming so hard that his mouth was foaming.

One of the officers said he really felt bad for Chelle and the things that Ty had put her through. He said that she looked like a bright young lady from a good family, and she probably didn't deserve the trash that he had brought into her home. He told her that with charges ranging from murder to statutory rape, Ty would probably be put away for a long time. Since the only evidence they had that Ty was sleeping with Mia was her pregnancy, they would have to wait until the baby was born for DNA testing.

When Chelle called Zora and told her what had happen, Zora hadn't scolded her or said I told you so. She didn't laugh or give Chelle any grief about what happened. All she said was, "Gimmie ten minutes to get there, Chelle. I'm on my way."

DONISHA

§

Donisha had been spending so much time with Marcus that she hadn't been to work at Brown Sugar since the night she made things right with Franko's spirit. Marcus worked as an accountant for a publishing company during the day, and he did a bit of teen counseling at the church on some evenings. The time that he had available to spend with Donisha was usually at night after work. Those hours happened to be when she was expected to be onstage, so she found a new job at a Marriott hotel cleaning rooms during the day and even enrolled back into college. She felt as if things were finally looking up for her, and for the first time in her life she could see herself with a future.

She had been busy cleaning all day. She was off from the hotel and knew that as soon as Marcus was off from work, he would be there. The whole apartment was tiled, one of the more unattractive elements of public housing for Donisha. Ed was sitting in front of the TV watching SpongeBob SquarePants, and Frankie was in her bedroom coloring. As Donisha mopped down the hall, she heard faint whimpering coming from her room. When she stuck her head in the door, Frankie lay in a crumpled pile in the middle of her bed. Donisha walked over to the bed and sat on its edge. She began to stroke her daughter's back as the whimpers became soft cries.

"What is it Frankie?" She asked in a gentle voice.

"I miss my daddy," she replied with a quivering voice. As if it were instinct, Donisha slid the child over to her lap and began to rock her.

"I know you do baby. I miss him too." Donisha could feel her eyes becoming glassy as she continued, "I miss my daddy too, but him and your daddy are together and they watch us every day."

"They were good friends, mommy Nisha," Frankie added in a sleepy voice.

"Yes they were," Donisha said as her own tears began to fall.

When Frankie fell asleep, Donisha noticed that she was clutching a piece of paper in her hand. Donisha pried the paper from her daughter's tiny grasp and turned it over. It was a picture. The picture was taken in Donisha's parents' living room. A wide-smiling Franko sat on the couch with Frankie sleeping comfortably on his lap. Donisha's father sat with a soft, congenial look on his face a few feet away from Franko and Frankie in his La-Z-Boy recliner. None of them were paying attention to the camera; the picture captured their genuine bond in this candid moment.

Donisha lifted the picture and put it to her lips, "I'm trying, daddy. I'm trying my best to make you proud."

When Marcus knocked on the door, Ed knew exactly who it was. He ran to the door before Donisha made it out from her bedroom. She laid Frankie down and pulled the door closed. She didn't want her to wake up, because the last person Frankie wanted to see was Marcus. Frankie didn't give Marcus a hard time, but Donisha knew that his being around was hard for her.

"Hey baby," Marcus greeted her as she walked down the hallway. He handed her a dozen roses and kissed her on the cheek as she fell into his chest to embrace him.

"Thank you Marcus. You always know how to brighten my day." Marcus's eyebrows creased in confusion.

"Is something wrong Donisha?" He followed her as she broke from their embrace and headed toward the kitchen to put her flowers in water.

"No, it's just that Frankie's having a hard day. She just cried herself to sleep, because she misses her father." Donisha watched Marcus's face for his reaction. His eyes told her that he was genuinely concerned.

"I hate to hear that, and I'll be praying for God to mend her broken heart." He looked at his watch and then back and Donisha before stating, "I just stopped by to tell you that I have a meeting at the church tonight, so I won't be able to stay."

Donisha tried unsuccessfully to hide her disappointment by busying herself with the flowers and the glass of water she was putting them in. Over the past few weeks she had managed to get very close to Marcus. She could talk about everything with him, and she never had to find a babysitter for her kids, because they didn't go anywhere that the kids couldn't go. He involved them in everything. He had even managed to get Frankie to smile at him a few times.

Sensing her frustration, he walked up behind her and slid his arms around her waist. His warmth was comforting to her, and she surrendered to the urge to lean her head back against his chest. "Baby, I know that it's easy to get frustrated with my schedule, but one day soon I'll be around so much till I get on your nerves."

Donisha turned her body around so that she faced him, "I've been lonely for so long Marcus that I know I'll never tire of your company."

Marcus sank into her lips so passionately that for a minute she thought that they would finally take it to the bedroom. All the kissing and caressing was wearing Donisha down. She was used to getting what she needed from a man exactly when she needed it, but with Marcus things were different. He respected her and her body, and sex just wasn't a big issue with him. She had decided to wait it out with him. He'd get it when he was ready.

He pulled away from her and chuckled out loud, "You know what woman? A pout from you is the least of my worries. I gotta go in here and tell Ed that I can't stay and play video games with him." They both burst into laughter at the thought of how her son would react to Marcus's not staying over. Marcus trudged across the tile floor toward the living area where Ed was and suddenly turned back to Donisha. "Oh, and my mama wants for you to call her." Donisha's eyes questioned him, and he shrugged his shoulders. "I don't know baby. She really likes you, and with her there's no telling what she wants," he said before disappearing into the living area.

Donisha decided that she would call Mrs. Black later that evening. She put the glass of flowers on her dining room table and walked into the living area just in time enough to see Ed's disappointed face turn from Marcus and plod down the hall toward his bedroom.

Marcus looked at Donisha with regretful eyes and shook his head, "I guess I'm not his hero anymore."

Donisha looked down the hall toward the door that Ed had disappeared behind. "He'll be OK, Marcus. He's just getting used to you being around. You go take care of what you need to."

Marcus leaned into Donisha and kissed her gently on the forehead. "See girl, that's why I'm falling in love with you." He paused to read her eyes. "You are so understanding." Donisha acted as if she hadn't heard his confession, but she had. And she had heard it loud and clear.

Three hours later, Ed was still locked in his room. Frankie sat at the kitchen table with one of her many coloring books while Donisha prepared dinner. Donisha jumped when the phone rang. It hadn't rung all day, and the fact that it still existed hadn't even occurred to her. Her phone activity had decreased quite a bit since all of her friends seemed to have men. Jamie would call weekly to check on her, but she rarely heard from the rest of her crew.

"Hello," she spoke into the phone.

"Hello, Donisha Raines?" The fast-talking male voice had to be a bill collector. Usually Donisha would lie and say she wasn't there, but she was tired of running. She let out a sigh and replied, "Yes, this is Donisha. How can I help you?"

It wasn't until the man said his name that Donisha realized who she was talking to and exhaled with relief. She couldn't understand why those people scared her to death, but there was something about bill collectors that made her cringe.

"This is Paul over at the Marriott. How are you today?"
"I'm good Paul. How about yourself?"

"Well," he began, "I'm doing fine, but I find myself in a bind over here. I know that your schedule usually consists of days, but do you think there is any way that you could come into work Friday night? Consuela is scheduled to work, but she had her baby today, and I really need that spot filled."

Donisha answered Paul with a "yes" before she even really thought about it. She needed the extra money because school was starting again soon. Ed and Frankie both needed new clothes and supplies, so all the extra hours she could get good would come in handy. She made a lot less money than when she was on stage, but she didn't have to gyrate on strangers' laps or take her panties off for extra cash anymore. When Donisha thought about it, she knew that her work at Brown Sugar had stemmed from greed, ignorance, and rebellion against her parents. Since she had moved out of her parents' house, the only bills she had were her phone bill and cable bill. Even before that, her parents took care of everything. During the short period that she had lived with D'Edward, Donisha became used to fast money and didn't want to work hard for anything, but now she hardly saw stripping as easy money. She wished that she could tell her father that she was sorry.

The ringing phone woke her in the middle of the night. When she looked over at the clock and it read 3 a.m., she knew that something was wrong. She picked up the cordless phone that sat on the nightstand next to her bed and answered with a groggy "hello." All she heard was sniffling before he blurted out, "Donisha, mama had a heart attack, and they say she won't make it." He started crying out loud, and Donisha didn't know what to say. She wanted to allow Marcus to get everything out before she spoke.

"Marcus, honey, calm down. I know that this is hard but I need you to tell me some things so that I can get there and be there for you."

He was quiet except for his sniffing, and then he said, "I knew I could call you; I knew you'd understand." He told her what hospital his mother was at, and she told him that she would be there as soon as Chelle came by to drop her off so that she could get her mother's car and leave the kids with her. He thanked her again and hung up.

Chelle had been asleep but agreed to come and get her as soon as she called.

The memories of the night when her own father died flooded her mind as she waited for Chelle.

Neither Donisha nor her siblings had been prepared for the Bishop's death. Mama Raines had known that the cancer was eating away at his liver for months. It wasn't until the night he died that she told her children. She said that their father wasn't the type of man to claim any sickness and telling his kids that he had cancer would be doing just that. By the time they found out, they all knew that he would die, but he didn't want anybody by his side except for his wife and his youngest child. Donisha's mother pulled her to the side before they walked into her father's room hand in hand.

"Baby, your daddy's happy to be going home." She looked down to hide her tears from Donisha. "I just don't know what Ima do without him. I didn't tell you baby. I wanted to so many times, but he said that I had to learn to accept it myself. He said that I still have to live when he's gone. He says that the kids will learn to live easy, but he worries about me." She looked at her daughter with pleading eyes, "Donisha, I know you ain't God, and you really don't know, but do you think I can make it without him?" Donisha nodded her head feeling pity for her mother as she put her hand on the doorknob to enter her father's room.

She had had a big job dealing with her mother's grief right after her father's death, and all she could think about now was Marcus's dad and what lay ahead of him if his wife didn't make it.

When she walked into the room, she saw Marcus standing beside the bed looking down at a sleeping Mrs. Black. Mr. Black was asleep in a chair beside the bed, and man dressed in scrubs was in the room as well. When Donisha entered the guy in the scrubs was resting with his arms folded against the windowsill close to where Marcus was standing. As soon as Marcus saw her, he ran over and embraced her. "Thank you so much for coming, Donisha. Mama will be glad to see you when she comes to." He let her go and turned to the guy who had now stepped away from the window and said, "Terrance, I would like for you to meet the woman in my life. This is Donisha."

Donisha smiled warmly at Terrance and shook his hand. Terrance offered a forced smile and eyed Donisha head to toe before he nodded his head. He didn't say anything, but Marcus hadn't seemed to notice his odd behavior. Donisha took in his appearance and found Terrance to be anything but attractive. He was neat and well-groomed, but his eyes stuck out of his head so far that he reminded her of an underweight fly. His lips were overly large—almost swollen—and discolored as if they had been burned by a chemical or drug. She could see him being friends with Marcus, because Marcus's looks had to compliment his where the ladies were concerned.

"Uh," Marcus began, "Terrance is an orderly here, and he called me when momma and daddy got here." Tears began to well up in his eyes as he looked over at his sleeping father. "He was so upset; he couldn't even remember my number. If she don't make it, I don't know what we'll do."

Donisha reached out and pulled Marcus into her arms as he let go of his emotions and cried openly like an infant. She had been so busy consoling him and he had been so upset that neither of them noticed when Terrance slipped out of the room.

After Donisha had been there for about thirty minutes, Mrs. Black's eyes began to flutter open. Mrs. Black looked over at her son and smiled. She opened up her mouth and strained out the words, "My baby."

Donisha could see Marcus's tears and held his hand tight to let him know that she was still there. His mother's words were faint whispers, "Marcus, I love you son, and God does too. Don't worry about nothing. He knows what happened confuses you, but he's gonna bring you out." A single tear fell from her eyes, and she continued, "I know what happened, baby, and it wasn't your fault." Marcus broke down and bent down and kissed his mother's cheek.

"I'm sorry, mama. I'm so sorry. I wanted to tell you, but I didn't want to see you hurt." Mrs. Black smiled at her son and rubbed the back of his hand. "Shhhhh, baby. It wasn't for you to tell me. Don't worry, I know and God's got it all under control. He's the only one who can help you anyway."

She moved her eyes over to Donisha and smiled, "I wanted to talk to you before I left. Marcus really does care about you baby and no matter what happen with ya'll, that much will always be true. Be his friend, baby. Even if it hurts you, I need you to be his friend." Donisha nodded her head and sank inside Mrs. Black's smile as she mouthed the words, "your father," to her only son.

ZORA

§

Ever since she'd shown up at Emory's house with a piece of pie that screamed the word truce, Zora and Emory had been inseparable. Zora had reintroduced Emory to Chelle. She thought that it was a good idea for Chelle to take her mind off of what had happen with Ty by diving back into school and using Emory as a mentor. The two of them clicked instantly, and Zora found herself just a tad bit jealous of their connection. She felt so out of place when right in the middle of one of her "why I love Alice Walker's, *The Color Purple*" speeches, Chelle shifted the conversation to the Robert Redford movie, *Legal Eagles,* and why it's one of the best lawyer flicks in history. Zora had never even seen *Legal Eagles*, so she sat quietly for ten minutes while they recited lines and laughed at jokes related to the movie that she didn't even find amusing.

Emory sat in the passenger seat of Zora's car as they drove from Nordstrom. They had just finished a little shopping at NorthPark Center. He was scheduled to leave for Africa in just three short weeks, and he and Zora had taken care of just about everything that was needed for his journey.

"Hey, let's stop by Chelle's and see what she's up to today," Emory suggested out of the blue. Zora looked over at

Emory trying unsuccessfully to hide her frown. She saw the bemused look on his face and quickly smiled to cover her disappointment.

Zora loved Chelle to no end, but Emory was beginning to represent something special in her life and she just wasn't ready to share that. Zora had never in her life truly been friends with a member of the opposite sex. She felt just as comfortable with Emory as she did with Chelle, Donisha, Kyla, and Jamie. Within the past month, Zora and Emory had had innocent sleepovers, dinners, and trips to the movies. They talked to each other and poured out their souls as if they'd die the next day. She felt a closeness to Emory that she didn't feel with her girlfriends, and she felt that sharing his friendship with someone would change what they had.

Emory had noticed her frowns many times at just the mentioning of Chelle's name but had refrained from mentioning it to Zora, because he hadn't wanted a repeat of what happened after he voiced his opinion about Will. Now he couldn't contain himself any longer. He had to tell her what he felt.

"Zora, I see that look every time I mention Chelle. What is it? You can talk to me. Tell me, what's up?"

Zora kept her eyes on the road and shrugged her shoulders as if she didn't know what he was getting at. "What look, Emory?" She took her eyes off the road for a second and looked over at him with a smile that she hoped would fix everything.

Emory looked at her in amazement. He couldn't believe that after the bond that they had built with one another that she would still attempt to hide her feelings from him.

"Zora," he began, "You have become something so much more to me than a friend, sweetheart, but that in no way makes me exempt from where God has me with my heart." He put his hand over on Zora's leg and squeezed gently. "Chelle needs someone right now. She is going through a very trying ordeal. It's like the world has been placed on her shoulders, and I respect her so much for what she is taking on. I want to be there to support her. I want us to be there to support her."

Zora didn't reply to him. She wasn't being stubborn or anything, she just wanted to wait until the car wasn't moving so that he could understand her, and she could let him know that she finally understood him.

"Hey," she began as they pulled into her driveway, "stay over for a while, will you? I'm gonna put together some rosemary chicken, and I want to talk to you."

Emory nodded relieved that his friend hadn't felt that his statement didn't warrant a response.

After Zora seasoned and put the wine- and rosemary-covered chicken in the oven, she poured herself and Emory a glass of white wine and joined him in the den. Emory stopped eating the popcorn that Zora had made long enough to take the wine glass from her hand. His eyes were focused on the television, which he had turned to CNN the minute they'd walked into the house.

"Hey," he said with his eyes still on the television, "Karen and Stacy had a little get-together last night. When you left to go pick your friend and her kids up, I decided to take my jog before you came back." Zora's eyes went up with interest as Emory continued. "You know, I usually jog on that side of the street on my way back, so when I past their house, there were all kinds of weird sounds coming from the backyard." He finally peeled his eyes away from the news and looked at her with a chuckle. "I didn't really believe you when you told me what you saw over there, so I went over to the gate and hollered over to make sure that they were OK. Well the short one—Stacy, I think—came to the gate and opened the door as wide as she could. She was stark naked and so was everyone else in my view." He looked toward the ceiling as if he were trying to remember something. "I saw three women all off into each other, and they never even stopped to look up. When I say they were all off into to each other, I mean it too. Tongues and juice were flipping and flopping from one set of open legs to the next."

He sat shaking his head with a strange smile on his face

before continuing. "What got me though is there was a guy there—and instead of him handling his business, Karen was handling hers on him with a strap-on. What was weird though is that while Stacy opened the gate with pride spread across her face, when Karen saw me there, I could tell she was humiliated. She looked like she wanted to pull that thing out of that guy's butt and run away. He probably would have been pissed though. His face told me that he was having a ball." He looked at Zora and shrugged, and they both frowned up their faces and finally laughed. "I guess that's where all those weird sounds were coming from."

Zora calmed her laughter and looked at Emory who was still shaking his head in disgust. He knew just how to lighten the mood, and his little story had done just that. Before she knew it, her mouth was open.

"Emory," she called to him to get his full attention.

"Hmmm?" he looked over at her and waited. He knew she had something on her mind and was eager to hear it.

"You were right that day. I was selfish, and I did think that my pain was far worse than anyone else's involved. You know, up until today I still couldn't see it. You had to bring to my attention that you were more concerned about my friend's well-being than I was." She was trying hard to hold back the tears that were building up. "I was just feeling so selfish Emory. I wanted something that was just mine and nobody else's. In my eyes, Chelle had her mom and dad. I just felt like I needed you more. Thank you so much for saying what you did. From this day forth, I promise to work on my heart."

Emory slid close to Zora and wrapped his arms around her. "I know it gets hard Zora, but I want you to know that you are a very special person to me. This is just the beginning for us, sweetie. I want to be here for you, with you." He cupped her face in his hand and wiped the tears away with his fingers. "And I want you to know that there is nothing wrong with your heart; God isn't through with you yet."

The next day at work Zora thought about the things that she had told Emory that night after dinner. She was tired and bored with her job as a professor. She had been elated when the university offered her tenure after her two-year fellowship there. She was sure that was what she wanted to do with her life then, but all that had changed after Bryan. It was as if the feeling had hit her suddenly. One day she woke up to get dressed for work and hated to go. At first she thought that it was just a phase and it would pass, but it hadn't. She didn't understand it. She had a very good job. It was what she'd always wanted to do. She had being feeling unsettled lately, though. She wanted a family; she wanted kids—she wanted a life. She had her friends, but she still felt alone. She had her job, but she still felt unfulfilled.

Ever since Bryan, things had been all wrong in her life. Zora hated him. She hated to even think of him.

Emory had told her that maybe God was preparing her for what her life was going to be. He'd said that the only way that he could probably get her to move forward when it was time was to let her see that she had nothing to loose.

After she'd lectured her first two classes, she left for the day telling her assistant to tell her last class that she was sick, but that class would resume on Wednesday. As she drove toward her house, her cell phone rang.

"Hello," she answered after she saw Kyla's name on the caller ID.

"Hey, girl," Kyla began, "we are all supposed to be meeting tonight at The Den. We haven't all hooked up in months except for in passing at church. Is that OK for you?"

"Yeah, that's fine," Zora responded, happy to have plans with her friends. "So, what's been up with you? I haven't talked to you since you babysat Ed and Frankie for Donisha a few weeks ago."

"I know, girl. You know my patients keep me busy." She paused and Zora sensed hesitation in her voice when she continued. "I—I broke up with Mike, Zora."

"What?" Zora asked truly concerned. "What did he do, Kyla?"

"Nothing Zora—that was the problem. I got tired of that dead-end relationship and decided that I'd move on." She sighed and added, "Now he calling begging all day, talking about how we were good together. Girl, I can't date a man with a past like his anymore. I mean Mike is a good guy, but he has one of them pasts that just ain't going nowhere. Besides, I was still noticing his white-collar hustler mentality at times. That promotions crap wasn't bringing in a dime." She laughed out loud before adding, "Ain't no telling where he was getting all those gifts. I mean damn girl, that man stole a credit card processing machine!" Her voice became serious again as she stated, "It's time for me to think about Kyla and her future."

"Good for you, Kyla," Zora said, "I am so proud of you for thinking of yourself."

"Promise me you won't flip out if I tell you something," Kyla demanded in a childlike tone.

"What is it, Ky?" Zora asked with concern.

"Promise, Zoe!" Kyla almost shouted.

"All right, dang girl. I promise," Zora chuckled.

"I been seeing Peter," she stated flatly.

"Huuuuhhh, Peter?" Zora asked to make sure she heard Kyla clearly.

"I think I might be falling in love with him, Zora," Kyla was serious.

"How?" Zora asked, still a bit shocked from the news.

"I don't know. He hired me as his nurse, but he really needed a friend. You know that." Zora could tell that Kyla was smiling now. "Peter's a handsome guy, so he meets plenty of women, but he's always honest and up-front about his disease. His honesty was the first thing that I ever found attractive about his character. Anyway, I get the calls every time they dump him. I'm his ear, and he's mine. The last one that dumped him, she was beautiful. Some model from New York. Perfect bronze tanned skin, bleach blond hair, and blinding white teeth. That bitch spit on him when he told her. He doesn't even kiss someone without letting them know, but she spit on him like he had deceived her." Kyla let out a long, heavy sigh.

"I don't see a death sentence when I look at him. He is my best friend. You know why you didn't know about me and Mike breaking up?" She answered her own question before Zora had a chance. "Because Peter was my shoulder to cry on. This is different from anything I have ever felt. This is the first time that love hasn't been about sex. He makes me a better person, Zora."

"Wow, Kyla! Anything that I could have flipped out about doesn't matter now. You have let love find you, and who would I be to judge that? I'm happy for you, sweetie. Peter is far from a loser. I'm happy for you," Zora responded.

"Phew," Kyla exhaled. "You have no idea how good it feels to hear those words. Thank you for being a friend. Well anyway girl, I just wanted to call you and let you know what was up for the night. I gotta go cause Peter is waiting for me, so I'll see you tonight."

Zora hung up the phone, happy for her friend. She always thought that Mike was a bit of a loser but never mentioned it. She was truly happy for Kyla and Peter. After her conversation with Kyla, she smiled all the way home.

Zora and Donisha arrived at The Den first, and since it was Tuesday night the crowd was thin. Zora hadn't even changed out of her denim Bermuda shorts and baby-doll shirt that she'd worn to work. Donisha looked nice, and for the first time to Zora, she didn't look trashy. She wore a dark brown wrinkled camisole blouse with a pair of light brown twill slacks and brown sling-back open-toed sandals. Her makeup was modest, and her hair was micro-braid free. She wore it short and spiked up at the top. The look became her, and Zora couldn't stop telling her how good she looked.

Chelle walked in twenty minutes after Zora and Donisha and walked straight over to their regular table.

"Hey girls," she began with a lighthearted laugh, "I had some trouble getting out here tonight, but I'm here." Before Donisha had a chance to ask Chelle what the trouble was, Zora pointed to the door at Kyla and Jamie walking in. Zora and Emory were the only people besides Chelle who knew what was going on with the situation with Ty. Emory had thought it wise to keep it a secret until everything was final.

The five women were so happy to be in each other's company, and for once in all the years that they had gone out together, they didn't mention men. Zora noticed that Donisha talked about her kids more than she ever had before, and Zora talked about leaving the university. Chelle talked about getting back on track with school, and Kyla talked about the rising rate of AIDS in the African American community. Jamie was the only one who just sat and smiled at her group of friends. They paid no attention to the men that tried to get their attention. Handsome or ugly, every brotha that walked into the place had scoped out the table of beautiful women who all seemed to be in a world of their own.

After they ate their dinner and talked all they could, they said good-bye. As they walked out of The Den with Jamie in front, she turned to her friends and smiled, "Looks like we've all grown a little in the past few months ya'll." The others just looked at her perplexed, because they hadn't even noticed that the focus of their night was different from any other. They didn't notice that for the first time ever they were truly happy with just being themselves.

CHELLE

§

Chelle had been fishing around her freezer looking for something to prepare for dinner when she heard the knock on the door. She stood frozen but not from the cold that came from the fridge. She had been living in fear for almost two months. Although she hadn't been bothered by any of Ty's friends or family, she was still afraid that this was the day that it would happen. She was tired of watching her back every time she walked in or out of her apartment and had started the search for a new place to live. She'd spoken with her parents about the move since she did live on a stipend from them. While her father was indifferent about her sudden change after spending six years in the same apartment, her mother was inquisitive.

"Why would you want to leave such a comfortable place after such an extended amount of time Rachelle?" Chelle thought fast, because she didn't want to worry her parents with what had gone on with Ty. She knew that if they knew what happened they would feel as if she were incapable of making adult decisions and would treat her like a child. They would want her to move home, or they would want to be there to supervise her constantly.

"I just feel as if it's time for a change, mother. Plus, I've started noticing a few thugs hanging around here. I just don't feel as safe here as I did six years ago." With that, her mother's eyebrows went up, and Chelle knew that she wouldn't ask anymore questions.

Ty had tried to call her collect four times the other day. She couldn't believe it. The first time she answered the phone, the automated voice alerted her that the call was from Travis County Jail. He had the nerve to announce his name when prompted. Chelle did not wait for the automated voice to ask her if she would accept the call. She slammed the phone down on the cradle as hard as she possibly could, but she was not surprised when it rang again. She picked it up, and right after the automated voice finished its message, he shouted as quickly as he could, "I'm sorry babe, answer th—," Chelle hung up again, but that idiot kept calling. Chelle knew that if Ty was calling her, then he was calling somebody else, but she hoped that those calls had nothing to do with a plot against her life. She stood paralyzed in the kitchen, because she wasn't sure if it was Vonita on the other side of her door waiting to pick a fight because she blamed Chelle for Ty's incarceration or one of his friends waiting to knock her off because of their loyalty to Ty. She was sure that he had spread the word that she was responsible for him being locked up.

"Who is it?" she spoke in a loud yet meek voice.

"It's Mia, Chelle." Chelle could hear the tears in the young girl's voice, and she rushed over to unlock the door.

As soon as the door was open, Chelle was sorry and proud at the same time of how she'd turned Ty in. Mia's once caramel-colored face had black and purple bruises all over it. Her left eye was swollen shut, and she had a torn pillowcase wrapped around her arm like a sling.

The child fell into Chelle's chest and cried as soon as she crossed the threshold of the apartment. She could feel her own tears running as she stroked Mia's back and tried to comfort her. "I am so sorry, Mia. I am so sorry, I didn't mean for you to get hurt." She guided the girl over to the couch and sat her down.

Chelle could now see the little pooch under Mia's small T-shirt and thought about the baby. She allowed Mia to cry while she patted her back for what seemed like hours. When the child finally dozed off and went to sleep, Chelle went into the kitchen and ran water over the steaks that she had sat on the counter earlier. She fried them and made baked potatoes to go along with them. By the time she finished setting the table, Mia was awake.

Chelle sat beside her on the couch and took her hand.

"Mia, sweetie, I need you to tell me what happened." Silent tears rolled down Mia's face as she looked at Chelle.

"You. You told, and they took him away. I wasn't even mad. I was happy, but I was scared." Chelle was quiet during Mia's pause, and Mia played with her fingernail as if it was the most important thing in the world. "It was about two days after the clinic. When I came in from summer school, mama was high and Darrell, Tyrone's brother, was with her. She was real mad, but he was even madder than she was. They were yelling and screaming about Ty being locked up, and mama said that child welfare had come by asking about me and my situation."

She started crying, and Chelle waited until she was done. "She slapped me and told me to go to her room. I went in there cause I always listen to mama, but after I was in there I heard her lock the door from the outside. Later on I heard the door unlock, and I thought she was coming to let me out, but it was Darrell. He came in and didn't say nothing. His eyes were real red and he was barely walking straight. I thought mama was passed out somewhere, but she wasn't. I sat up on the bed and Darrell came over and pushed me back down. I tried to slide off the other side but he pulled me up and slapped me. When I fell back on the bed, he held me by the neck and started tearing my clothes off." She paused and started sniffling like a child does when she can't stop crying. Chelle put her hand on her shoulder and let her get her pain out.

"He put his nasty thing in my mouth and my butt as hard as he could. My nose was bleeding and blood kept coming out of my butt. I was waiting for mama to come in and hit him in the head or something, but then she came in and sat in the chair next to the bed and watched." She was crying out loud now, and Chelle was patting her back like a baby.

"How did you get out Mia?" Chelle asked full of concern.

Mia tried wiping her own tears away, but they kept rolling down from her blotchy, swollen eyes. "I don't know how long I was in there, but it was ever since that day. After that first day I heard them talking through the walls about how child welfare would be back. Darrell went out and stole a lock, and they put me in the bathroom. The only time they let me out was when he wanted to put his thing in me, and after that they would give me noodles and water and put me back in the bathroom. Last night when he came to get me, I was ready. I hit him with the shower curtain rod right in between the legs, and when he screamed she ran in there." She paused and smiled as if she'd just thought of something funny.

"She ran in there to protect him when he cried, but watched while I was in pain. She let him have me and beat me every day, and she ran in there to protect him. I hit her in the head with the rod, and when she fell, I ran. I had left your address at school in my locker, so I slept in the park, but as soon as the school doors opened, I snuck in and got your address."

Chelle managed to smile through her tears, glad that Mia had been able to get away.

Mia looked at Chelle and sighed, "I just wanted to stop by and say thank you."

Chelle hugged the girl so tight that she thought she would break her.

"Let's eat cause I'll bet you're starved and then we're gonna get you to a hospital."

DONISHA

§

Mrs. Black's funeral was extremely hard. Even at Mr. Black's age, he didn't know a lot about making arrangements, so a lot of the burden of that task fell on Donisha. She didn't mind. Her heart went out to the Blacks. She knew what it was like to lose a parent, and she had seen how difficult it had been for her mother when her father died. Her mother was a big help with the funeral arrangements as well. She had called Sandra Clark Funeral Service from Dallas to come down to Austin and handle the services. Donisha and her mother purchased Mrs. Black's clothes and shoes for the service and instructed the funeral directors on her hair and makeup.

When Marcus was driving her home the night before the funeral, he grabbed her hand and brought it to his lips.

"I'm so glad that I found you, Donisha." She smiled softly as he continued. "God changed my world when he put you in it. I don't know if you'll ever understand how important you are to me, but Dad and I are grateful, and we owe you forever for all that you are doing for us right now."

Donisha quickly shook her head. "You don't owe me anything. Neither of you. I am right where I'm supposed to be and doing exactly what I am supposed to be doing." She tilted her head and gazed thoughtfully at him as he kept his eyes on the road.

After a short pause, she said, "I don't think you'll ever realize how much you changed my life. I can still feel myself changing now. Marcus Black, I'm glad you found me too.

After only a few weeks both Mr. Black and Marcus were still taking Mrs. Black's death pretty hard. As soon as Donisha got off from work, she'd pick the kids up from her mother's and head to Marcus's parents' house. Marcus hadn't gone to work since his mother's death, and he insisted that Donisha drive his truck. She was grateful because that meant she could come as soon as she got off work without having to ride the bus. He had expressed to her that he didn't want her to have to wait for her friends to get off of work to get a ride herself, and he sure didn't want her catching the bus.

She'd cook them dinner and make sure that everything was clean before heading back home. Marcus wasn't ready to go back to his own apartment, so he'd been staying with his father. His father would sit in front of the television until he fell asleep. He said that he just couldn't sleep in his bed without his wife.

So this day was no different. After a long day of changing sheets and cleaning toilets in hotel rooms, she drove over in Marcus's truck to his father's house. When Donisha knocked on the door, nobody answered. She pounded a little harder and waited for a response. There was no answer, and she turned away puzzled. The two men hadn't left the house since the funeral. She wondered where they were, and her wonder became worry. When she turned to walk down the steps with Ed and Frankie on her heels, Marcus stood in front of his truck with the first smile that she had seen on his face in weeks.

"I got a surprise for you woman," he leaned down to hug her. "Me and daddy been talking about a way to thank you for all the kind things that you've done, and we found one.

Come here," he said pulling her toward the barn behind the house.

He was pulling her so fast that she had to look back to make sure that the kids were still behind her. "Marcus, where's your father?" Donisha asked now out of breath.

As soon as the question passed her lips she turned her head and almost ran right into Mr. Black. Even he had a smile plastered across his face, and that brought tears to Donisha's eyes. Just last night he had been a mess and here he was now all smiles. For a second she thought that Mrs. Black's death had taken them both over the edge and they had lost their minds, but when Mr. Black stepped aside Donisha couldn't do anything but cry.

"You like it?" Marcus asked with a voice full of enthusiasm. Donisha was speechless. "We traded in mama's old car and bought it for you. You don't even have to worry about the insurance. We got it all taken care of."

She couldn't believe it. At almost thirty years old Donisha had never owned a car and now somebody had given her a brand-new one. She opened the driver's side door to the black Ford Explorer. She heard the kids asking whose truck it was and heard the proud responses from Marcus and his father.

Donisha covered her mouth as she turned around to face the men from inside the car. She dropped her hands and hugged Mr. Black, crying "thank you" the whole time they embraced. He pushed her away gently, holding on to her arms. "No, baby girl, thank you. You have been an angel to this family. We just wanted to let you know that we appreciate you. Anyway," he said with a distant look in his eye, "I know Berta Mae woulda wanted this."

She looked over at Marcus, and he was still smiling as he watched the kids climb inside and explore their new vehicle. When Donisha walked over to where he was standing, he looked down at her and wiped the tears from her eyes with his fingers. She fixed her lips to say thank you and he put his fingers over them.

"I want to be here to give you anything you need, baby. I love you, and I love Ed and Frankie, and when ya'll go without, a part of me goes without. Donisha, girl, I know you're my rib and I don't have to wait any longer because I know I love you now." Donisha covered her mouth with her hands as Marcus got down on one knee. "I know I'm in love with you now. Donisha Raines, will you make me the most blessed man alive and be my wife?"

Donisha couldn't speak; she just nodded her head and wrapped her arms around Marcus's neck while weeping into his chest.

Donisha was almost done cleaning the Blacks' house. All she had to do was go upstairs and clean the bathroom. When she walked out of the kitchen, she froze at the sight she saw. Ed and Mr. Black were in the corner of the den concentrating on a game of chest. Frankie had been sitting on the floor drawing a picture, but she was now headed toward the couch where Marcus was sitting flipping through channels with the remote. Aside from laughing at a few of Marcus's jokes, Frankie hadn't responded to him well at all. She'd always made sure she kept away from him. When Marcus saw her headed his way, he dropped the remote at his side and made his usual attempt to converse with Frankie.

"What cha got there, beautiful?" he asked with a smile. He almost fell out of his seat on the couch when she answered.

"I drew a picture for you, Marcus." He gasped and put his hand on his chest, "For me?" She climbed on the couch and sat right on his lap and began to explain the picture.

"This is me and Ed, and we're a playing in your daddy's yard, but sometimes I get sad because I miss my daddy. When I look up to the sky right here," she said pointing to the upper part of the paper, "my daddy is smiling and telling me not to be sad. He is saying that it is OK to be your friend because he knows your mama and that you are a good guy. You and mommy Nisha are here on the porch swing watching us, but you can't see my daddy." She stopped and looked up at Marcus. "Do you think that it is really OK for me to be happy and my daddy's gone away?"

Marcus sighed, trying to suppress his urge to cry and shook his head, "Frankie, sweetheart, your daddy's not gone away," he pointed his finger at her tiny chest. "You carry him right here every day."

And just like that she was pointing her little finger all over the paper and didn't even notice that Marcus was wiping his tears. Marcus didn't know that Donisha was watching and wiping tears of her own.

ZORA

§

Zora was shocked to see him on the other side of her door. The only reason that she had opened the door without looking out the peephole was because she knew that Emory would be back any minute now. He had just run home to get some onions, because Zora didn't have any in her house.

"What do you want?" Zora asked exasperated without letting him through the door.

Bryan tried to look past Zora into the house. "I'm here to see my child. Did we have a boy or girl, Zora?" He was looking at Zora with what she saw as a smirk on his face, as if he was actually serious in some sick way.

"Bryan, I want you off my property or else I'm calling the police," she stated flatly as angry tears started to well up in her eyes.

"Zora, if you call the police, I'll just head down to the attorney general's office and put myself on child support. You think you can keep me away from my child?" He was gritting his teeth, and Zora could see the frustration in his eyes, but he took a few steps back.

"Look Zora, I'm sorry about what happened. I really am. I can't make excuses for who I was then, but I'm a better man now. I'm a good man now. I just want to be a part of my child's life." His head was hung, and for a moment Zora felt bad for him. It had been over a year since the last time she saw him, and she could tell that he had just come out of the darkness that had engulfed him. His appearance was different from that day. His face had been sunken and ashen. His lazy eyes were even lower that day, and the scraggly hair on his face and head grew wild. His once medium frame had become small and frail, and back then Zora had known that she couldn't save him.

He was different now as he stood before her. He was the Bryan who held her when the detectives had shown up and told her that her parents had perished in the fire at their camping cabin. He was the Bryan that had wiped the sides of her mouth when she couldn't stop throwing up after the detectives left. He was the Bryan that had loved her to no end before he became the Bryan that had so deeply hurt her. He really didn't know what had happened, and it was Zora's responsibility to tell him.

Zora had been so elated about the baby even after she'd found out about the drugs. When Donisha told her that he used to come by the club and snort coke with some guys every now and then, she had been willing to accept the fact that he did drugs socially. She knew Bryan loved her, and he would stop when she asked him to. Plus from what she'd heard, coke wasn't very addictive. Bryan had been there with her through so much. He had stood by her side through the tragic loss of her parents, and she couldn't walk away from him after that for such a minor thing.

It wasn't until she'd found the empty crack vials in his pockets that she'd become worried. When she'd asked him about them, he said that he had sold the crack from inside the vials and left them in his pockets by accident. The argument shifted from the empty vials to him selling drugs. Zora and Bryan had made a deal at the beginning of their relationship that he would stop dealing. She had helped him get a job at the university as a janitor and thought that he had stopped selling drugs. After the argument he promised to stop selling drugs and leave his hustler mentality in the hood.

Bryan had been happy about the baby too, but Zora had noticed a change in his attitude as the months went on. By the fourth month of her pregnancy, Zora was preparing to become a single parent. She wanted badly for Bryan to come around, but he would go for weeks at a time without calling or coming by. When he did come by he would be smelly, hungry, and high. It didn't take long for her to figure out that Bryan wasn't the drug pusher. She knew that he was using and that he was far past a stage where she could help him out.

Bryan's sister called her one day to tell her that Bryan couldn't come around anymore, because he had stolen his mother's television. He had even been fired from the university for coming to work high. Zora was glad that none of her colleagues knew about them. At least it saved her from possible embarrassment at work. But nothing could save her from how hard she was on herself, for still loving such a loser.

It was late one night in her seventh month that Bryan came by and changed her heart. As usual, he was smelly, hungry, and high. After he ate the dinner that she fixed for him, he walked into the living room where Zora sat and stood over her. "I need some money, Zora."

Zora looked up at him with tired eyes and shook her head, "No, Bryan I'm not giving you money. I know what you need, and I will not help you."

Zora became afraid by the look in Bryan's eyes as he pulled her up from the couch by her shirt and began to yell in her face. "Where's your purse, Zora? I need some money." Zora had put herself in the habit of hiding her purse two months ago when she started to notice money missing. The spittle that gathered at the corners of his mouth almost made her want to get the purse and just give him the money that he was begging for, but she loved him too much to help him kill himself. He was the father of her child, and she knew that somewhere past the drugs he was a good man.

She wasn't expecting his fist when it smashed against her jaw. She lost her balance hitting the coffee table before she landed on the floor on top of her life-filled stomach.

When she came to, it was over. No baby or Bryan.

By the time the paramedics got Zora to the hospital, it was too late for the baby. They did an emergency C-section and because of the hemorrhaging that Bryan's kicks had caused, an emergency hysterectomy.

Bryan hadn't even returned for baby Zari's funeral and Zora had cursed him and hated him for the void he'd left in her womb and her heart. Bryan fled from Zora's life that night, taking with him all the money she had in her wallet and leaving her with a broken jaw, an empty and barren womb, and a broken heart.

Zora looked at him with pity and said, "Bryan, I'm sorry, but you and I don't have a child." Bryan shook his head and when he looked up Zora saw that he was on the verge of tears.

"Zora, I'm sorry. I really am. I can't blame anyone for what I did to you, but God forgave me. You are a good person, and I know you got a good heart. Please let me see my child."

Emory walked up and Bryan moved aside to let him by, while trying to hide the tears that flowed from his eyes. Zora knew that Bryan had changed. A year ago he would have been all over Emory, and now he stood aside and let another man pass him and go through a doorway where he truly believed he had a child inside.

"Bryan," she began, "I'm sorry for what happened too. I've been so mad, and up until now I really thought I hated you. But now I know I don't. Bryan, I am sad for you, so sad for you." Emory stood beside Zora and when he saw tears fall from her eyes, he placed his hand on her shoulder.

"It was too late when they got there," she blurted out, "We had a little girl, but she never opened her eyes." She paused as Bryan's silent tears became loud cries. "But I don't hate you, Bryan; I forgive you. I know that you didn't kick me. It was the drugs. They took my baby, they took my womb. Just tell me, Bryan. Tell me you beat em."

Zora saw Emory disappear into the house as Bryan fought to control his tears. "I thought about the baby every day, but that thing had me so strong until I couldn't get to her." He looked off toward the street and continued. "I really did love you Zora. I don't want you think that it wasn't real. I just wanted to get myself together before I came to see the baby. You always deserved better than me and I'm glad you got him," Bryan said nodding his head in the direction of the doorway where Emory had reappeared behind Zora. Zora didn't attempt to try and explain her and Emory to Bryan. She was still shocked by his being there.

"Here you go man," Emory stepped passed Zora and handed Bryan a paper towel. Bryan looked up at Emory and smiled, "Thanks man." After he wiped his tears with the paper towel, he stuck his hand in his back pocket.

"Oh I forgot, Zora. I can't give you back everything that you lost because of me, but I can give you this." He handed her a small white envelope and added, "You don't have to open it now." Zora nodded her head in agreement. "Zora, I know that this could never be enough, but for everything," he paused and looked at the ground when his eyes welled up again, "everything I ever did to hurt you, I'm sorry."

Zora surprised herself when she walked up to him and embraced him. Emory looked at them and smiled as they held each other and cried. He knew that Zora's selfishness had stemmed from a hurt that was far more painful than what Will had done. She had needed this closure with Bryan to forgive all men for what he'd done to her.

Zora watched Bryan as he turned his back to walk away and yelled out to him, "How'd you do it Bryan? How'd you give up the drugs?"

Bryan looked back and smiled, "I didn't. He called my name, and I heard him. God called my name, and I heard him." With that he turned back around and got into the small, old car he was driving and left her life again.

When Zora turned around to walk back into the house, she remembered the envelope in her hand. When she tore it open, she found the 100 dollars that he took from her purse the night he destroyed their baby and her womb.

All that she could hear as she walked in her house with Emory close behind her was his voice saying, "I really think that brotha's going to be all right."

Emory didn't ask any questions about who Bryan was or what had happened, but Zora was pretty sure that he had figured it out. They went on about the rest of their day as if the incident with Bryan hadn't happened, but Zora couldn't hide the relief that she felt. When she'd hugged Bryan, it was as if a huge burden had been lifted from her shoulders, and she found herself wanting to thank him for giving her the chance to forgive him.

"What are you gonna be up to while I'm gone?" Emory asked the day before it was time for him to leave. They had been cleaning Emory's house every since Zora's classes had ended earlier that day. They sat on his porch and drank lemonade.

"I'm thinking about offering my resignation while you're gone," she stated without looking up at him. "Today was the last day of summer semester, and I just don't think I wanna go back next year. Seems like all I ever wanted was to be offered tenure; now that I have it, I'm ready for something else." She looked at her hands before continuing, "I think that's life though. You reach your goals to create new ones. You don't stay put; you move on."

Emory was quiet for a while and then he spoke: "I think you're right. I think you're so right, Zora." He paused and looked at her seriously, "I think you have more than that to think about while I'm away too."

Zora looked up at him, puzzled, and asked, "Think about what Emory?"

Emory looked down at Zora and offered the same sincere eyes and warm smile that he'd been giving her for the past two months. "Zora, I'm gonna be honest with you tonight. I don't know what to expect when I get off that plane in Africa. I may never come back, but I'm willing to risk my life if it will save others." He took a sip of his lemonade and sighed, "I've watched you change in so many ways, and I can't help but feel proud of who you are becoming. I would love to look down on you with the eyes of a big brother and pat you on your back." He looked out into the yard at Gideon who was now yelping at another dog running by the house with its owner. When the passersby disappeared around the corner and Gideon was quiet again, Emory continued, "But I can't Zora. I can't look at you like that because I want to look at you through the eyes of your man, your best friend." Zora looked up at him from her lap where her eyes had been focused.

He continued, "I love you Zora, and I don't need you to say anything tonight. I want you to drop me off at that airport tomorrow and think about it for the whole thirty days that I'm gone." He took her hand in his. "If you want me Zora, I want you to be sure. I don't want you being with me just because you feel alone. I'll be here. We're friends and no matter what, we'll always have that." With that said he stood up and pulled Zora to her feet. "Come on, Zora, let's take this dog for a jog."

The next day when they pulled up to the airport and Emory put his hand on the door handle, Zora stopped him, "Em, wait." He turned to face her keeping his hand on the handle. "What's up?"

"I can't have kids," she looked down at the steering wheel. "I thought you heard me that day outside with Bryan, but I guess not. I can't have kids."

Emory opened the door and smiled, "I heard you, Zora. We'll talk when I get back. See you in thirty days." With that he leaned in and gently kissed her on the forehead and was off on his journey to save the world.

CHELLE

§

After the doctors in the emergency room examined Mia, they called the police right away. Reluctantly, she repeated her story, and she and Chelle waited for results to the tests the doctors had ran.

They sat in the room that Mia had been put in for observation.

"I don't want this baby," Mia blurted out, "I can't keep this baby, Chelle." She looked at Chelle with pleading eyes.

"I know, Mia. We'll take care of it. We'll go back to the abortion place in the morning if that's what you want." Mia looked into Chelle's eyes.

"I can't just kill it anymore," she said with a faint smile, "I felt it move while the doctor was with me," her smile faded. "But I'm too young, and I won't keep it. I don't want to be like her. Can't I sell it or something?" Chelle shook her head no.

"You can put the baby up for adoption when it's born," Chelle corrected her.

"Well then that's what I'll do." Mia sat back in her seat satisfied with her decision.

A few minutes later the doctor came in and told them that the baby was all right and that Mia would be under observation for the remainder of the night. They found out that Mia was a little closer to five months pregnant than four, and the doctor had made her an appointment with a nearby OB/GYN, because her young age made her a high risk pregnancy. He told Chelle that she could wait for child welfare or come back and say good-bye to Mia before they took her away in the morning. Chelle chose the latter because she felt that she had some heavy thinking to do, and plus she needed to shower and change clothes.

On her way out of the hospital Chelle was stopped by a police officer. "Excuse me, miss," he said while tapping her on the shoulder. When she turned to face him, Chelle recognized the officer that had given her the information on Ty at her house that day. She smiled at him warmly, letting him know that she recognized him.

"Rachelle right?" he asked.

"Right," she answered.

"You're just the person I was looking for. In case you've forgotten or I didn't tell you the last time, I'm Officer Royce Briggs. I just came back from Mia Carter's home, and I got some information that you might want to know," he paused as if he had an idea, "Would you like to have a cup of coffee with me?"

"Sure," Chelle answered, eager to know what was going on.

They got on the elevator and rode to the sixth floor where the cafeteria was.

Chelle watched the officer closely as he ordered his coffee after her. She hadn't noticed that his features were so agreeable on the day of Ty's assault. He reminded her of Steve Harris from the Tyler Perry movie, *The Diary of a Mad Black Woman.* He had the same bald head and full lips.

"So," he broke her from her trance, "we meet again under more tragic circumstances. Truth is my shift ended right after I left the Carter house, but after I saw your name on the police report I came right over hoping that you'd still be here."

Chelle nodded her head for him to continue.

He shook his head before saying, "When we got there, the mother was sitting on the couch with a needle in her arm. She was dead. Overdosed. We found the boyfriend hiding in the closet, and I'm pretty sure that when the DNA samples are tested they'll match whatever has been taken from the girl." He lowered his head and shook it again. "What is this world coming to? How is the girl?"

Chelle shook her head and answered, "She's shaken up and alone in the world, but I think she'll be OK."

"It's the saddest thing to see, but I see it more than I'd like to admit. Child welfare will take her and place her in a group home where neither she nor that child she's carrying will have a fighting chance." He looked up at Chelle and asked rhetorically, "But hey what can ya do?"

Chelle was quiet for a moment, and the officer eyed her pensively as she sat thinking.

"I think I'm going to keep her, Officer Briggs," She said as if she had just made the decision, "I think I'll keep her and the baby."

His eyes grew wide with wonder, "Keep her? Do you think you can handle that?"

She nodded her head, "Sometimes we need to sacrifice ourselves for the benefit of others." Her eyes glazed over with tears, but none fell. "My Aunt Mattie used to say that people come into your life for a reason and you never know what God is gonna do for you or have you do for them."

He sighed and leaned back in his seat, "You'd better get up there so that you can tell child welfare about your plans." As she pushed her seat back and stood up to leave, he spoke again.

"I knew the first time I met you that you were a good woman." He took a sip of his coffee and smiled. "But you didn't drink your coffee. You still owe me that cup of coffee." Chelle smiled and nodded her head as she made her way back to the elevators so that she could go claim the motherless child.

It had taken hours to get the temporary custody paperwork signed, but when it was time for Mia to check out, it was all done. Chelle had called Zora and asked her to stop at the store and buy Mia a change of clothes. As they sat in the room and waited for Zora's arrival, Mia stared out the window.

"Why you doing this?" she asked not making eye contact.

Chelle looked at Mia and saw a frightened little girl with no one in the world, sitting there wondering why someone would help her.

"Because you deserve it, Mia. Everybody deserves to be given a chance to be somebody." When Mia turned back to Chelle her eyes held a pool of tears.

"Thank you. Thank you for telling, thank you for bringing me here, and thank you for taking me." She looked down at her hands and then back up at Chelle. "What do you want me to do?"

Chelle looked at her confused and asked, "What do you mean?"

"How do you want me to pay you?" Mia asked as if Chelle should have already known what she meant, "I'll cook and clean and wash clothes. I'll earn my keep. I really will."

"No, baby," Chelle said shaking her head. "I just want you to be a child Mia."

Over the next couple of days, Mia and Chelle settled into their life together quite comfortably. Chelle had hastened her search for a new apartment knowing that Mia needed her own room. She found a nice two-bedroom condo in a good, safe neighborhood close to her old apartment.

Ty had called collect and of course Chelle didn't accept the call. She didn't let it bother her, because she was moving and would change her number the following week. She had told Mia about her mother's death and was surprised when Mia cried. She had patted the child's back and comforted her so much in the past few days that it had become second nature. Mia and her mother had been cut off from the rest of their family because of the drugs when Mia was two years old, so as far as she was concerned she didn't have anyone. A local church had donated money to buy Mia's mother a coffin and she had been buried without services.

Chelle began to pack up her apartment, and Mia helped. Chelle couldn't help but grow attached to the girl because she was such a good kid. She had been exposed to a life that Chelle had never imagined and of course the effects of it lived inside her. Chelle had seen Mia stick food under her shirt from the refrigerator when she thought Chelle wasn't looking and she'd also seen her flinch a few times when she moved toward her too fast. Aside from that she was the sweetest kid in the world. She was tidy and always picked up after herself. Chelle had to tell Mia on several occasions that it was OK to leave a few dishes in the sink and that she'd wash them later.

Mia didn't have any clothes; Chelle took her shopping the day after they left the hospital. Mia had been so easy to please, always replying to Chelle's question of, "Do you like this one," with, "only if you can afford it." Chelle bought her ten maternity shirts and six pairs of pants from the Gap. She bought underwear, bras, and socks, and even bought a pair of Nikes, flip flops, and slippers. She took Mia to Sears and bought her three pajama sets and called Donisha to get the number of the girl that used to braid her hair. The very next day Mia was sitting in Banta's chair getting the five-hour hairstyle that would last her for the next four months.

Chelle hated leaving Mia alone while she went to her internship after having skipped three days to stay with her, but she was working at a firm that her school had set up for her and she didn't think it wise to skip another day. She left Mia with all possible numbers to get in contact with her.

She worried about her so much that day that she called Zora and asked her to go check on her. She knew that Emory had gone to Africa and since summer school was over, Zora was free. Mia had met Zora and Emory a few days after she was there. Surprisingly she had taken really well to Emory.

Chelle had expected her to shy away from Emory because of what she had been through with men and had warned him and Zora before they even came over. After everyone was introduced, Mia was real quiet. Emory, Zora, and Chelle started talking about Emory's upcoming trip and when he'd replied to Chelle's question of, "What will they do with all the orphans?" with "God has a special place for all of his children and whether we see it fit or not, he knows just where they need to be," she sat down beside him and began to ask him questions.

Even though Zora and Chelle were having a conversation of their own, Chelle still remembered Mia's curious questions.

"Does God really love all of his children?" Mia asked. Emory looked at her with sincere eyes and answered, "Yes, Mia. We just have to remember that we all have different crosses to bear. Everyone's is heavy in its own way, but it'll never be too heavy for us to carry. Have you ever heard the saying 'God will never put more on you than you can bear?'"

Mia shook her head no and lowered her eyes so that she was looking at her hands resting in her lap.

She had been quiet for a minute before asking, "So, why does he let some kids have such a hard time in life?" Chelle knew that that question had been about her own life, but Mia had been too broken inside to say it.

"Well," Emory began, "God allows tragic lives, like those kids have, to happen so that he can give other people a chance to be as special as they are. I think those are the ones that God loves the most, and the only time that God really notices the people that seem to have it all together is when they let the special ones see him through them."

Mia's eyes had tears in them and she tried to wipe them with the sleeve of her shirt.

"Do you think he loves me?" she asked.

Emory was having a hard time holding back his tears when he reached out and patted her hand and said, "I know he does, Mia. I know he does."

When Zora called back and said that no one would open the door, Chelle left the firm and sped home. When she drove up she saw Zora sitting inside her car in the visitor's parking space. Zora hopped out of her car and met Chelle at her front door. When Chelle opened the door to the apartment it was quiet, and she didn't see Mia anywhere. She called her name loudly as she ran toward the stairs and Zora fled to the kitchen. She heard a doorknob click before she reached the stairway and turned to see Mia coming out of the coat closet. Her face was wet with tears as she cried, "I'm sorry, Chelle. I didn't mean to scare you. I heard the knocking, and I thought that they were coming to take me away."

Chelle ran toward Mia and threw her arms around her, "Nobody's gonna take you away from me, honey. Nobody has a right to."

Mia was sniffing loudly, "I thought that they made a mistake and mama was alive and not dead. I thought they were coming back to get me. I'm sorry I didn't mean to scare you."

Chelle pushed Mia away from her and held her by her arms, "I'm sorry for leaving you alone, Mia. I'm sorry for scaring you."

Zora, who'd been standing in the doorway of the kitchen watching, chimed in, "OK girls, from now on during the day, Mia you stay with me."

Chelle smiled and nodded her head as she thought about the adjustments that she was ready and willing to make in her life for Mia's happiness.

DONISHA

§

What's done in darkness will surely come to light!" Pastor Leo screamed from the pulpit. Donisha sat in between Zora and Chelle and some young girl Chelle had brought with her. Kyla sat in the last seat on the row with Peter right beside her. She was becoming used to the amens and hallelujahs that came from her friends' and her own mouth. Church had become something different for them all. No more were the Sundays where that talked like children until it was time to go. She looked down at her friends to see them all giving Pastor Leo their full attention. She could see Marcus sitting on the front row next to Jamie. He hadn't been sitting in the pulpit for about a month. He'd said that he had some things to work out with God and until they were cleared, he refused to sit up there.

"Ain't nothing you can do and hide it from the Lord!" the Pastor screamed while wiping the sweat from his forehead. Donisha knew that this was the end of his sermon, because the louder that he got the closer he was to closing. "Don't you know that thing that you battled yesterday is the same thing that somebody needs to hear about today. Somebody say amen," he commanded, still screaming. When the amount of amens coming from his audience was insufficient, he waved his hand as to shoo the congregation and said in a much lower voice, "Awh, ya'll don't know what I'm talking about." The amens were louder this time, and he screamed again, "That same demon that tried to take you out yesterday is trying to take somebody else out today. God didn't allow you to go through that thing to be embarrassed to talk about it, church."

The Book of Hebrews says Jesus Christ the same yesterday, and today, and forever.

Pastor Leo wiped the spittle from the corners of his mouth before continuing, "He loved you when you was out there on dem streets, he love you now that you in here praising his name, and he gon love ya when he see ya in his father's house."

He lowered his voice as the organ began to play. "Tell that thang, ya brethren in need."

After the services ended, everyone met outside like they did every Sunday. When Zora suggested that they all go out to dinner, everyone agreed this time. Donisha and Marcus and the kids followed Zora; Chelle and that young girl got in Marcus's truck. Kyla drove behind them with Peter and Jamie in her truck. When they were seated in Zapeta's, they caught up on each other's lives while waiting to be served.

"So," Zora began looking in Donisha and Marcus's direction, "What's been going on with you guys." Donisha blushed a little bit before putting her hand out in the middle of the table for her friends to see her ring. Zora covered her mouth with both hands while Chelle smile warmly. The ring fit Donisha's personality exactly; it was effortlessly beautiful and unique—a two-carat, pear-shaped diamond solitaire on a thin platinum band.

"Oh my God," Zora said, "You're getting married?" Donisha nodded her head as Chelle and Kyla said almost in unison, "Congratulations, Donisha. I'm so happy for you." Jamie didn't say anything, but she smiled. She had talked to

Donisha earlier that morning before church, and Donisha had told her then that she was engaged.

"When is the wedding?" Zora asked still surprised that her friend had finally met Mr. Right.

Marcus spoke before Donisha could, "She won't set a date, ya'll. Please talk to her."

Donisha gently slapped Marcus on his back, "We don't know yet, but I'm working on that. I just want things to be perfect and that includes our wedding date." Donisha looked over at Chelle and the girl, "What about you Chelle? What's been up?"

Chelle looked at Mia and smiled at her as if she was a cooing child. "Nothing, I have a new roommate, Mia," she said looking toward her. "She ran into some problems at home, and she is going to live with me now." Donisha and Kyla's eyebrows shot up, but they didn't dare ask any questions for the sake of making Mia feel comfortable.

"Well," Kyla held her hand out and let her friends see the giant rock flashing on her ring finger. "I'm getting married too," she stated as her eyes roamed the table for her friends' reactions. Zora let out a scream this time, "Oh my God, Kyla, you weren't playing were you? You guys are in love!" Kyla's smile remained on her lips as she shook her head no.

"Good ole Mike." Donisha said with a smile.

"Nuh uh," Kyla shook her head.

"Then who?" Chelle asked puzzled.

"Peter," Kyla said as she put her hand on top of his. She saw the expressions on her friends' faces go from excited to perplexed, and then to accepting. "I know what you guys are thinking," she began, "but Peter is perfectly healthy." She looked at Peter and smiled. "He is not dying from AIDS. Peter is living with HIV." Peter lifted her hand to his lips and kissed it.

Donisha didn't want to sound ignorant, but she had questions, so she asked, "But doesn't someone that has HIV get AIDS sooner or later?"

"Donisha don't d—," Marcus began, but Peter put up his hand to stop Marcus from hushing Donisha's question.

"No, Marcus, man, it's OK. Some people really don't know this, but people with HIV can live the rest of their lives without actually contracting AIDS. It's about taking care of yourself," he paused, looked at Kyla, and continued, "And believing in God." He looked around the table and smiled, "When I first found out five years ago that I was HIV positive, I thought that it was the end of my life. And when my family found out, they thought it was the end too. I was only twenty-four, and there I was preparing myself for death. A lot of people think that it's a disease that affects only gay men or drug addicts, but it's not. That didn't stop people from calling me a fag or thinking I did drugs. I contracted HIV from a long-time girlfriend, and she had contracted it from an ex-boyfriend." He looked at Kyla's friends. He knew that they were hearing his story for the first time, and he wanted them to understand.

"It was really hard at first. My family wanted nothing to do with me and gave me money to stay away from them." He smiled and said, "But they're coming around now since they understand more about the disease. I thank God for Kyla. Without her I would have been alone in this battle. If she'd never brought me to church I wouldn't even know a God to thank. I come from a family of Scientologists, and they truly believe that our bodies are inhabited by other beings." He looked around at his audience and let out a lighthearted laugh.

"I thank God for HIV, because as tragic as it seems, it brought me to him."

After dinner, Donisha rode over to the Blacks' house with Marcus. She was going to pick up her truck and clean up Marcus's apartment. He was ready to go back home but had commented on how his apartment was a mess. His father was at his chess table playing a solo game and looked up and waved at Donisha with lonely eyes. Donisha still felt bad for Mr. Black. After being married for thirty-five years, he was alone. She walked into the den and kissed him on the cheek before she left.

She stopped by her mother's house to drop off the kids and went inside for a little while. Her mother was in the kitchen shelling peas when she got there, and Donisha sat at the kitchen table in front of a huge angel food cake. Her mother made it a point to always have some kind of baked good acting as a centerpiece on her table. Donisha had called her and told her mother about Marcus's proposal, and her mother had been so excited for her.

"Mama," Donisha said while cutting a slice of the cake, "what is it like to be alone after all that time? I mean you and daddy were married for forty years. I know it must be hard."

Her mother turned around from the sink where she had been shelling the peas. "It gets easier every day, girl. It gets harder every day too. I lay down at night and I think I made it another day without him, but I wake up every morning and think, I can't make it today without him. It's a struggle, but what about life isn't?" She put one hand on her hip and tilted her head to the side and a thoughtful look graced her face.

"Bout a week fo yo daddy passed he said to me 'wife, if anything eva happen to me, I want you to live. I want you to respect that God thought it not yo time, but mine. Don't die wit me, live fo me." She looked over at her daughter and smiled.

"And that's just what I try to do. So them days when I wake up thinking I can't make it witout him, God drop his words in my spirit, so that's just what I do. I live for the both of us." Donisha nodded her head thoughtfully and stood with her cake in her hand. Her mother turned back to the sink but called out to her just as she was walking away, "Donisha, what makes it easier is the memories. The good ones and the bad ones. I hold on to the kisses and the fights with the same tight grip. The fights is where we gathered our strength and experience. The kissing is where we built up each other." Her mother looked up at her from the bowl that she was using to shell the peas and stared deep into her eyes.

"I keep the agreeable and the not so agreeable parts of your father in my heart. That way he'll always be with me. The real him. For better or for worse."

Donisha let her mother's words sink in before announcing that it was time for her to go.

"Well mama, I'll be back as soon as I'm done." She kissed her mother and left for Marcus's apartment.

When she pulled up at Marcus's apartment, she had to park in the visitor's spot, because there was an old, red Toyota parked in his spot. When Donisha got to his door, a man was standing there with his hands on his hips tapping his foot as if he was waiting for the door to open. His back was to her and he was facing the door, so Donisha didn't recognize him until he turned around as she approached him. She immediately recognized him and smiled as she came closer. It was the funny looking orderly from the hospital the night of Mrs. Black's death.

"Terrance, right?" she said with a smile and her hand held out to shake his. Seeming irritated, he looked down at her hand but didn't attempt to shake it. She felt uncomfortable, so she blurted out the answer to a question that hadn't been asked, "Marcus isn't in there."

He flared his nose at her, "I kinda figured that out already. I was coming to talk to him about something, but since I see that he really is giving out engagement rings, I can talk to you." Donisha's brows went up as she looked down at the hand that he was pointing at.

"What can I do for you?" Donisha asked with a bit of aggravation in her voice, losing her patience with this little funny-looking man.

He reached down and stuck his hand in a small canvas bag similar to a purse or tote; which was leaning up again the porch. He took out a videotape and handed it to Donisha.

"What is this?" she asked, fed up and now slightly concerned.

"Just watch it, you might learn something, honey," he said as he picked up the bag and walked away. He hustled over to his car, got in, and drove off without looking back.

Donisha watched as his small car turned the corner and drove out of her sight. She shrugged her shoulders and unlocked Marcus's door.

Upon entering the apartment she smelled a putrid odor. It smelled like something had died in there, and she was surprised that the cops weren't surrounding the place. She put her keys in her purse and sat it on the coffee table along with the tape that Terrance had just given her. She followed the stench, which led her straight to the kitchen. When she looked into the sink, there sat a pack of chicken so green that it reminded Donisha of money. Marcus had complained that something was stinking in his apartment each time he came over to get clothes, but Donisha guessed that it had never dawned on him to look in the sink.

The apartment was as messy as it was dusty. After she cleaned the kitchen with a whole lot of bleach to cover the smell of funk, she dusted the rest of the apartment. The bedroom and bathroom had been the biggest tasks. It was horribly dirty, but Donisha still smiled at the thought of having a future husband who would leave the house looking like a pigsty.

She finished up in about an hour's time and it wasn't until she picked up her purse that she remembered the tape. She put her purse back down and picked up tape as she walked over to Marcus's entertainment center. He had a VCR and DVD player combo, so she stuck the tape in and hit the power button on the television. She didn't know what she was about to see.

When the tape first started, Marcus was standing behind the pulpit preaching to an excited congregation. He looked different, because he had more hair on his head and face. His face even looked a few years younger as it was free from the worry lines that now decorated his forehead.

Donisha watched and was interested, because she had never heard him preach before. She had always missed service that day, and even if she had been there in the past, she wouldn't have heard him. She would have been busy running her mouth with Zora, Chelle, or Kyla. Not Jamie though. She didn't miss a Sunday, Tuesday, or Friday service and was always front and center.

He was calm in his demeanor as he spoke to the church. He was preaching about holding on until it was God's time. It was a good message, and she was impressed with how well Marcus was doing. Just when she was getting into his sermon, the film cut off and changed to a bedroom scene. The bed was empty and quiet. She was about to eject the tape when she heard a voice coming from the video. The first person to walk in was Terrance. He looked happier than Donisha had ever seen him look. He was all smiles and excitement. Marcus walked in behind him and he looked sad and empty. It was as if Terrance was posing for the camera, and Marcus was unaware that it even existed.

Before Donisha could blink, Terrance was on his knees in front of Marcus unzipping Marcus's pants. Donisha covered her mouth with her hands as Terrance took Marcus into his mouth. She felt hot tears sting her face, and then the vomit came up her throat. She ran into the bathroom before it could reach her mouth.

After she had flushed the toilet and washed her hands and mouth, she stood in the mirror and watched the tears stream down her face. She wanted to wake up from this nightmare, but she couldn't, because she wasn't sleeping. She opened the door almost afraid to come out of the bathroom and walk through the living room past the TV to the front door.

She walked fast and decided that she wouldn't look in the direction of the TV, but as soon as she was in the room, her eyes went to the screen. Marcus was plowing away at Terrance's rear, and Terrance was screaming so high-pitched that he sounded like an opera singer. Donisha grabbed her purse and walked out the door, leaving the tape running and the door unlocked.

As she drove to the Blacks' house, her mind was clouded with thoughts. He's gay. He hadn't touched her in all their time together. She thought he was so holy and in love with God and here he was a homosexual. How could he use her like that? She wasn't some cover-up for what she thought was his sickness. And the church, no wonder he sat his tail down from that pulpit.

By the time she pulled up to the house, all of her hurt had turned to anger. She got out of the truck and saw Mr. Black over by the barn fixing the door. He hollered, "Hello," and she waved as she strode into the house to find his son.

He was sitting on the couch and when she walked in, he smiled. He stood up and walked toward her but stopped, trying to read her expression.

"You bastard," she screamed, "You gay bastard!"

He stood still as she continued to assault him with her tongue, "I saw the whole thing. Your little boyfriend brought a tape by your apartment."

His eyes welled up with tears, and he let them flow freely. "Oh, you gon cry now, huh?" she asked with sarcastic pity. "Should have known you would, you little bitch." She started to cry and he walked toward her, but she held up her hand and stopped him. "Keep your punk ass away from me, Marcus."

"I'm sorry, Donisha. I didn't mean for you to find out this way. There were so many times that I wan—," Donisha silenced him with her keys upside his head. They fell right at his feet, and his eyes followed them to the floor.

"I loved you, Marcus. I wanted to be your wife, and you were using me as a cover, you sick bastard. Why?" She began to cry again. "Why?" she screamed as she looked to him for an answer.

He removed his hand from the spot on his head where the keys had cut him and wiped the blood on his pants. "Donisha, baby, I love you more than I love anything on this earth. I would never do anything to hurt you."

She looked at him and almost sounded as if she was pleading, "Say it wasn't you, Marcus. Just say it wasn't you, and we can get past this. I'll believe you. I know that you aren't a loser. You can't be. Please just say it wasn't you, Marcus." She cupped her face inside her hands and wept as if she was there alone.

"I can't lie to you, Donisha. That was me on the tape, but I need you to listen to me. I'm not the same person that I was that day. Just let me hold you so that I can tell you about it, baby."

He began to walk toward her slowly but stopped when she lifted her head. Donisha pulled the ring off of her finger, struggling a bit to get it over her knuckle. After what seemed like forever, the ring finally budged and slid to the tip of her recently manicured nail. She let it fall to the floor, the facade making a dull thud on the hardwood.

"OK, Marcus. You've made your choice so stay the hell outta my life." She bent down to the floor and picked up her key, still bloody from its impact with his head. Standing erect again and bloody keys in hand, she turned to walk out of the house. While she was moving away from Marcus, she could see his tears flowing, but it didn't matter now. Marcus was gay, and that was the life that he had chosen.

ZORA

§

Spending her days with Mia was just about the only thing helping Zora readjust to life without Emory. He had called her when his plane landed in Africa, and then again after his first week there. His voice was different the second time he called. It was like he had seen things that left him in awe. They had only talked for ten minutes, but he described everything in intricate detail, from the people that had died to the babies that had been born. He was away from the camp for a few days to run some errands with Roy, and he said that was why he was able to call her. He said that there were no phones at the camp, and Zora's heart had sank, because she knew that that would be her last time speaking with him before he came home.

Mia was a pleasant girl who had been dealt a terrible hand in life. The first few days she was quiet as she tried to adjust to Zora's house. After that she began to open up and ask Zora about things that puzzled her, telling the stories of her life with her questions.

One day she sat on Zora's porch swing and watched her do her own pedicure. She observed her for a while before she asked, "Will you do mine too?"

Zora looked at her feet in the flip flops that Chelle had bought her and nodded her head, "Of course, Mia." She started back on her own before she asked, "Have you ever been to a nail shop, sweetie?" Zora asked. Mia shook her head no, and an idea came to Zora suddenly.

"Why don't we go to a real nail shop?" Mia's eyes brightened as she pondered the idea and then asked, "Isn't that real expensive?"

Zora stood up and began to pack up her little nail kit. "Don't you worry about that." She tilted her head to the side and looked down into Mia's eyes. "Looks like you could use some pampering, sweetie." Mia smiled, stood up, and wrapped her arms around Zora. Zora hadn't expected the hug, but it was a welcomed treat. It was rewarding to make the child smile with what seemed to her as such a small gesture. She wondered if that is how Emory felt when he did the wonderful things that he did for people. She wondered if he felt as proud at those times as she did when Mia smiled.

When they made it back from the nail shop, freshly polished and pampered, Jamie's red Jetta was parked in front of Zora's driveway. Zora hadn't seen Jamie since they all went to dinner last Sunday and was surprised that she was happy to see the car parked in front of her house.

"Hey girl," she said as she got out of the car. "What a nice surprise, huh, Mia?" she said turning her head to Mia. Mia nodded her head but kept her eyes steady on the ground when she was done, and Zora knew that she had reverted back to the quiet frightened Mia.

"Hey Zora," Jamie said with a smile in her voice. She looked over at Mia and smiled. "Hello Mia. We weren't formally introduced Sunday, but my name is Jamie." She stuck out her hand for Mia to shake and Mia took it and smiled back at Jamie.

"So, girl," Jamie began, "what have you been up to today?"

"Nothing really, girl. We just came from getting pedicures," Zora said showing Jamie her toes.

"Well, I just stopped by because this is where the spirit led me and I'm glad I did. I didn't know Ms. Mia would be here, and getting a chance to meet her is a real treat."

Zora could remember the times when she, Kyla, Donisha, and Chelle would see Jamie and the spirit coming and they would run the other way. Jamie had been a "sellout to Christ" Christian since the day Zora met her in college. She had introduced Jamie to Kyla because she had a cousin that was dying from AIDS and needed a nurse. They had welcomed her warm attitude into their group, but they grew tired of her always talking about God when they were talking about men, partying, or sex. Jamie was a mystery to them all, and though at times her "holiness" seemed to be a little over the top, they all knew she meant well. Jamie had been through a lot, and they all understood that holding on to the unchanging hand of God was her way of dealing with the demons of her past. In Zora's opinion, Jamie needed therapy, but she had known people like Jamie all her life and true to her experience, Jamie's reply was always the same, "Jesus is all the therapy I need."

Kyla had been the only one that seemed to really tolerate her prophesying and speaking in tongues every day, but on this particular day, Zora welcomed Jamie and the spirit into her home.

They walked into the house, and Zora fixed three glasses of lemonade. She sat the glasses on the coffee table and took a seat on the couch next to Mia.

Jamie took a sip from her glass and looked over at Zora. "I'm so excited cause now I know it was the spirit that sent me here, Zora. I woke up this morning with that child on my mind," she said pointing to Mia.

Mia's eyes grew wide, and she focused her full attention on Jamie and waited for what she was about to say.

Jamie looked at Mia and said, "God wants you to know that he's heard your cries and he knows your pain. He said that he does love you, Mia, and he has a very special place for you."

Zora sat shocked by what Jamie said while Mia's eyes ran over with tears. For the first time since Zora had met Jamie, she received her as a prophet.

Zora was surprised when she heard Mia's voice, "I knew he heard me."

Jamie smiled and nodded her head for her to continue. Mia stated simply, "I asked him to give me at least one person to love me, and he gave me more." Zora leaned into Mia and held her while she cried; she dropped a few tears from her own eyes.

Zora stopped by the mall on the Saturday after she visited Chelle and Mia's new apartment. Mia had told Zora that this was the first time that she had ever had a room of her own, and Zora wanted to find the perfect gift for her. She had grown so fond of the child in such a short time and just wanted to spoil her by giving her all the things she never had.

Mia's presence lightened Zora's pain from knowing that she would always be childless. In some strange way, she could feel her own deceased child Zari through Mia.

She didn't want to buy her clothes, because Chelle had been shopping for the girl nonstop. Zora could see happiness in Chelle that hadn't been there since she first met her at UT Austin. Back then Chelle was always talking about her Aunt Mattie. Zora thought that when her aunt died, a small part of Chelle had gone with her. Whatever Chelle lost had seemed to come back to life with Mia.

She went inside a new gift store in the mall and looked around. When she didn't see anything there, she went across the way to a Christian bookstore. She peered down every aisle, looking for nothing in particular. When she saw a large wooden sign that looked as if it were made for the outside of a church, she knew that she had found the perfect gift. The sign read in large, bold letters: *I Live Here.*

She was hungry after her purchase and decided to head to the food court. On her way she passed an athletic footwear store and went inside. She wanted to start jogging with

Emory when he returned, but she needed new running shoes. To her surprise, when she walked into the store, she saw an astonished Will. He had spotted her before she noticed him and looked as if he was ready to find a place to run and hide. It was only a matter of seconds before she understood why he looked so afraid. A short, petite young lady came from the other side of a display case and said, "Baby, I like those right there. I want those. Are you still gonna buy them for me?" She was a cute, young-looking girl, and Zora immediately thought of the wigged gorilla that Will had at home. Here he was out shopping with some Jada Pinkett Smith look-alike and his ugly wife was somewhere settling for it.

What a loser, she thought to herself.

He stood there wondering what Zora's next move was going to be. He was almost sure that his cover was blown, but she surprised him and herself when Zora turned around and walked out of the store.

Emory had only been away for two weeks, which was why Zora was surprised when he called her and told her that he was at the airport and needed for her to come and get him. She was elated that he was back but hoped that nothing bad had happened to send him back home before his time.

When she pulled up to the passenger pickup area he was standing there grinning with a few more bags than he had originally left with. Zora smiled hard as she parked beside the curb and jumped out of the car to help him with his luggage. When they embraced each other, Zora noticed for the first time what Emory's presence meant in her life. He was a true friend—not that her girls weren't true friends—but it was different with Emory. They shared a deeper friendly bond that was absent between Zora and her girlfriends.

"What are you doing here?" she asked as they loaded his things into the trunk of her car.

"What, you aren't happy to see me?" Emory asked with a smirk on his face.

She gently slapped him on the arm and replied, "You know what I mean, silly."

Once Emory placed the last bag in the trunk of Zora's car, he looked at her thoughtfully. "It's amazing how just seeing your face can make me forget all that's going wrong in the world." Zora blushed and lightly stroked the side of his face.

"I love you too, Emory," she replied sweetly, "Now let's get you home."

"Not before I get something to eat, Zora. I'm starving like Marvin," he said jokingly.

Zora suggested that they stop and get Chinese food on the way home, and Emory agreed. When they arrived at his house, take-out food in hand, Emory was euphoric. He said that he had only slept in a bed when he left camp for those couple of days when he called her.

"Things were a lot worse at the camp than I thought they'd be." His eyes looked sad for the first time since Zora had met him. Zora could tell that Emory hadn't shaved at all while he was away, because he almost had a full beard. His look was rugged and slightly unkempt, but it made him even more beautiful to Zora. He was different, but it was the type of different that was better. "I expected death, but I didn't expect to see people who were dead yet still alive." He looked at Zora with a serious expression on his face.

"Zora, our camp is near the Sudanese border in the Gambella region, and there are many restrictions on coming and going into the camp because of the raids and violence going on in Sudan. Those restrictions even apply to food deliveries, Zora. So as you can imagine, our camp and other camps nearby are suffering at critical levels of malnutrition." He placed his fried rice down on the table. Zora knew that he wasn't hungry anymore after he'd thought about the people he'd left that were still without food.

"That's not even the worst of it. Roy and I traveled to a Sudanese refugee camp when we were away from our camp. It was worse than our own. This camp had very little water, and there were no food deliveries scheduled for them." He stopped and sighed dejectedly.

"In December of 2003, the Anuak, a tribe in western Ethiopia, were blamed for the ambush and murders of eight government workers. Ever since then, the Ethiopian military have been committing horrendous mass murders and rapes against these unarmed civilians."

"That's terrible," Zora sighed.

"Well, that's why I came back. All of this is going on over there, and the media has no access. A few U.S. congressmen have signed a letter to Prime Minister Meles Zenawi, but we need a few more for him to really think about giving access to any journalist or human-rights organizations. This letter, if it pleases the prime minister, will allow media access through Ethiopia, so that people will be well aware of what is going on over there. It is more like a petition to issue a call for help. I have a few connections in Washington, DC, and I'm flying there the day after tomorrow to get the ball rolling on the signatures." He gave Zora a long hard stare before he continued.

"Some of the people that I met there really changed my life, Zora. They are beautiful and they are being wasted. I met this little girl, Dannae. She is only eleven years old, and already they call her "little mother." She gave birth to twins after she was raped and left for dead in a village raid. It's a wonder the children survived the attack. When Dannae was found, her breasts had been removed with machetes, and sticks were driven up her body through her vagina." Emory shook his head sadly. "Eleven years old. She walks on a cane and can't control her bladder, but you will never see her without those children strapped to her body. She doesn't smile much, but when you talk to her, she never stops bragging on how God spared her, so she must be special." His eyes became hard, and he swallowed.

"Our convoy was robbed."

Zora's eyebrows rose at his words.

"We were moving supplies from a food center to our camp on three trucks when rebels attacked us. We were driving on a road where there was nothing as far as the eye could see besides dirt. We had a very long way to travel. When the little boy jumped in front of the truck that my guide was driving, he was almost hit. There were about ten of them total, half boys and half grown men. Every single one of them had eyes devoid of humanity. They cursed and spat and even slapped around some of the members of our convoy. Everyone suggested that we give up our food, but I refused. After I spent a few minutes of arguing with one of the crazy rebel soldiers, he just hit me across the head with his weapon. He didn't care about my degrees, that I was American, or that you were here waiting for me. Roy said that he wanted to kill me while I was unconscious, but he settled for the food. My life is not worth a bag of lentils in Africa, Zora. But I love her. She is the most beautiful thing on earth. Africa, sweet mother Africa.

"I was afraid that your trip would be dangerous, Emory. Are you sure you want to go back?" Zora wished he would forget about nursing Africa and stay here with her.

"I'm going back to Africa because God has a plan for me there, Zora. Who am I to question it?" He looked at her with soft and loving eyes.

"I really missed you, Zora. I mean I missed you more than I imagined I would. I was around all these people that were desperate for my help. They needed me, but I needed you." They had been eating their food at the coffee table, so Zora scooted closer to his spot on the floor.

She draped her arm around his neck and placed her hand on his head. As she began to twirl one of his curly locks, she said with a smile, "It's funny, but this is the only physical thing about you that I recognize. You were almost perfect to me when you left here, Emory, and that's why I can't understand how you came back even better." She looked into the oceans of emerald green that were his eyes, and he leaned in and gently pressed his lips to hers. Five seconds felt like five hours as their lips touched. It was a beautiful kiss. Zora could feel the blood pumping through Emory's lips and for a moment she felt as if they were one person. It wasn't a bedroom-leading kiss but a sweet and lasting gesture that whispered to her, "I love you more than words can say." Emory and Zora both knew that at that moment, they were in the exact place that God wanted them to be.

CHELLE

§

Zora had been a lifesaver. Chelle really appreciated her for looking after Mia while she finished up with her internship. She was glad that by the time school would start back up Mia would be enrolled in alternative school while she was in school.

She had invited Zora to dinner as a way of saying thanks for what she was doing and was surprised when Zora told her that Emory was back. She couldn't help but feel that Emory was perfect for her friend. He was so down-to-earth and spiritual and just a good man that Chelle truly admired him as a friend.

She ended up inviting them both to dinner, so she and Mia went to the grocery store so they could prepare the perfect feast. Mia had become comfortable enough with Chelle to place a few items of her own into the shopping cart. Chelle was still worried about her and felt that she needed counseling, but Mia refused to speak with anyone about the pain she was suffering from. Even at the OB\GYN Mia was completely silent. She would answer question with yes and no answers but was unwilling to offer any detailed information. Chelle was surprised when Zora told her about what happened with Jamie, but it gave her hope and she knew that she would never give up on Mia.

As Chelle pushed the shopping cart, Mia walked beside her. Chelle tried to get her excited about going to a regular school after the baby was born, but she couldn't even get excited herself. It was unnerving to Chelle how they never mentioned the baby that Mia was carrying. When Mia wanted fried pickles, it wasn't a craving because of her pregnancy, it was just something that she had a taste for. When she realized that her pants were getting too tight, it wasn't because she was gaining weight from the growing baby, she was just getting fat. Chelle tried anyway. She loved the girl, and she just wanted to see her smile.

"It's gonna be so much fun Mia. We'll be able to do our homework together, and we can even ride to and from school together." Mia only nodded her head with her eyes still distant while holding on to the end of the shopping cart.

While they stood in line at the checkout, Chelle heard someone say her name. When she looked behind her, there stood Officer Royce Briggs. He was in his uniform and was holding one of those plastic lattice baskets with a few select items inside.

"Hey," he said before Chelle could say anything, "I thought that was you. Is this the lucky little girl that you rescued?"

"Yes," Chelle smiled, "This is Mia. Mia, this is Officer Briggs. He's the one that told me about your mother. Remember? I told you about the officer who came back to the hospital that night." Mia nodded politely and turned her head toward the front of the line.

"She's still a little traumatized," Chelle whispered to Officer Briggs so that Mia wouldn't hear.

"I totally understand." He paused and then stated, "So when can I get that cup of coffee?"

Chelle smiled while considering the idea of telling him that she would have coffee with him later but thought that it would be better to ask him to come to her house for dinner that night. He quickly agreed and asked her to please stop calling him Officer Briggs, she could call him Royce. She gave Royce the address of her new apartment, and he knew exactly where it was.

Chelle and Mia returned to the apartment, and Chelle went straight into the kitchen to put the groceries away and start dinner. Mia went into her room and laid down for a nap.

Chelle was busy in the kitchen doing everything from peeling raw shrimp to seasoning her famous hot wings when the doorbell rang. She was more than happy to find Zora on the other side, because she could use her help in the kitchen. She noticed right away that Zora was glowing. She wore her thin wire-framed glasses, which Chelle always thought made her look so sophisticated. Her hair was so bouncy and shiny; Chelle knew that she had just stepped out of the salon. The subtle yellow calf-length sundress complimented her tall yet curvy body frame, but none of those things had anything to do with her glow. The glow was in her big chestnut brown eyes. They smiled before she did.

"You look so cute, Zora," Chelle commented while eyeing Zora's dress and then looking down at her own yoga sweats and T-shirt.

"Thank you," Zora sang, "I feel good too. I felt so good I just decided to see how things were coming along. Oh, and did you get a chance to catch up with Donisha?"

Chelle nodded her head yes and added, "But she wasn't feeling up to coming over. I think her and Marcus might be fighting, because she smacked her lips big time when I mentioned her bringing him." Chelle led Zora into the kitchen, and Zora leaned against the counter as she watched Chelle slice tomatoes and mushrooms.

"Oh, I was just wondering. Anyway, Emory had a long flight so he said he'll be over later. I just wanted to come by early because I have something for my baby in the car. Where is she anyway?"

Chelle looked toward the back of the apartment. "She's back there taking a nap," she paused and sighed, "Zora, I am so worried about her. She's keeping all this stuff bottled up and I'm not sure what that can lead to. I just wish that she would talk to someone. She won't even mention the baby."

Zora was quiet for a second, and then she looked at Chelle with concern. "Maybe she just needs time, Chelle. It's only been a little over a month. I think that she's progressing well. You have to understand, Chelle, she's been through a lot to be so young. We don't know exactly what happened with her and Ty and the rape, and his brother and her mother's disregard for her well-being could have really pushed her. She may not want to talk about the baby, because it's a reminder of the pain that she wishes she could forget."

Chelle nodded her head. "OK, we'll see. Anyway, I have a guest coming for dinner." Zora's eyebrows went up and Chelle continued, "Remember the cop that I told you about? Mia and I ran into him at the grocery store this afternoon, and I invited him over. I thought it would be a good idea to let you meet him so that I could actually listen to your opinions this time." They both laughed at Zora's bad feeling about Ty from the start for the first time, and Zora understood why God had held her tongue on the *I told you so.*

As soon as Emory arrived, Chelle laughed at how Mia almost knocked him over trying to get him to come in and hang up the sign that Zora had given her. Emory greeted Chelle quickly as he disappeared behind Mia into her room. Chelle could hear him telling Mia about the children that he had encountered in Africa. She and Zora sat quietly on the couch while the TV watched them, and they listened to his interesting stories.

"I met one little girl who is just about your age, Mia. Her name is Tausif." It was quiet and then he continued, "She's pregnant too." Chelle looked at Zora hoping that Emory hadn't said the wrong thing. Anyone could see that Mia was pregnant, but it was always hard on her when it was pointed out.

"Tausif was kidnapped in a raid about two years ago. She was brutally beaten and raped by over fifty soldiers every day for eleven months until she barely escaped with her life. By the time she made it to the camp eight months ago, she had already contracted HIV from one of her captors and was pregnant. She doesn't know who her child's father is. She doesn't know who gave her the disease that is probably gonna kill her, and she doesn't even really have a place to live. Her whole family died in the raid, so she is alone." Chelle stood up and walked down the hall. She stood by the door just where she could see Mia attentively watching Emory as he positioned the sign and told the story.

"She doesn't know if her child will survive inside her, and she doesn't know if her child will be born sick. Tausif doesn't have medicine to fight off the AIDS virus that she is in danger of contracting, but she is so happy. One night after she sang to all the smaller orphans that she shares a tent with, I asked her, Why do you smile so much, Tausif? She smiled even bigger and told me, 'I smile because God loves me. Even if he never heals me and nobody else ever says they love me, I know he does because I am here.' With all the negatives in her life she still believes in God's love." Emory was quiet for a second, and then he said, "Mia, you're here."

Chelle could see Mia's tears and then she watched Emory open his arms like an eagle spreads its wings, and Mia melted into his chest. He rubbed her back, and Chelle heard him whisper to the child, "God says in his word that whatever you do unto the least of these, you do unto me. Mia, everyone who has hurt you has to answer to God."

By the time Royce arrived, dinner was ready. It was the first time Chelle had seen him without his uniform, and he looked really good. He wore a pair of Dockers with a yellow polo shirt and some very white Nike sneakers.

He surprised Chelle with a dozen yellow roses. It was the first time that a man had ever bought her flowers. Emory and Zora liked him. At the dinner table, they talked about everything from literature to the Iraq War.

Mia was quiet all through dinner and excused herself early, and Emory and Zora left shortly after they finished their meal. Chelle and Royce sat on the couch in her living room, and to her surprise, there was no uncomfortable silence.

"So, how is she doing?" he asked, nodding his head toward Mia's room.

"I'm worried about her, Royce. She stays cooped up in her room and refuses to talk to anyone about what happened. What really bothers me, though, is that she acts as if the baby doesn't exist."

Royce smiled warmly and nodded. "That happens a lot in these situations. I take that you have never run into things like this?" Chelle shook her head.

"No, I haven't. I mean, I've seen this kind of stuff on TV and even prepared a case at school about a similar situation, but I've never been this close to anyone that has been hurt like this."

"Well, I'm gonna give you a friendly piece of advice. Let God handle her pain. She's lost and confused. When she's ready to talk, she will. God knows." Chelle smiled and nodded her head.

"The funny thing is somewhere deep down inside I know that. My Aunt Mattie used to say that all the time."

It was after midnight when Royce left her house. He and Chelle had really hit it off. She found out that he was two years younger than her. He was only twenty-five, which shocked her because he was so mature. He was from Chicago, K-town to be exact. He had moved to Texas only a year ago when he was offered a job in a police department with a program where he could train to be a narcotics detective. He talked about God a lot, and that surprised Chelle considering his age. He said that he was raised in the church, but he was more spiritual than religious. When he'd admitted to not having a church home in Austin, Chelle quickly invited him to Victory and Praise. He'd kissed her on the forehead and promised her that he'd see her at church tomorrow.

When he was out of her door, Chelle smiled. This was the first time that she had ever had a man over to her place for dinner, and it didn't end in sex. No matter how young Royce Briggs was, something inside her told her that he was different.

DONISHA

§

The only reason she answered the phone was because she didn't recognize the number in the caller ID. When she heard his voice, she immediately wished she had let the machine catch the call. Donisha had been dodging Marcus's calls for weeks. She didn't even understand why he was still calling her. Ed had been grilling her every day about why Marcus hadn't been around, and Frankie had even asked about him a couple of times.

"Please don't hang up, Donisha," he pleaded with her, "I'm outside your door. Please open up. Just give me five minutes. There is something that I have wanted to tell you about since the moment I knew I was in love with you. Just five minutes, please."

Donisha sighed, "It's too late, Marcus. I found out the hard way. I already know you're gay."

"Please Donisha, five minutes."

"Marcus, you have five minutes and not a second more," she said as she flung the door open and stood in it letting him know that he was not welcome inside. She stood there for a minute with the phone still at her ear before she finally put it down.

"Donisha, I love you—,"

"Is that what you had to tell me?" she cut him off, "Cause if it is, you're wasting my time. You told me that before, but you showed me otherwise."

"I was confused, Donisha. I'm not gay." His eyes were sad but certain as he looked at her.

"Look, niggah, you said that was you in that tape sticking ole boy and if that ain't gay then I don't know what is."

"I got raped," his words were fast and sharp, and they silenced Donisha as she waited for him to continue.

"It was my sophomore year of college, and I was away at Texas Tech. I didn't know anyone except for the people that I met at school." He paused and held his head down, "There was this dude in my chemistry class that was real cool, and he invited me to a party real far out close to a lot of hog pens and chicken shacks. When we got there, I realized that it wasn't my type of crowd. It was a bunch of big country-looking dudes. Nobody from school was there, so I was ready to go. Ole dude had run off to one of the pens where they kept the hogs. When I looked in one of the pens, about five of the dudes where standing around watching this one dude sodomize a big hog. The hog didn't make a sound as the guy kept thrusting in and out of it. Then I was hit on the head from behind. When I came to I was tied up real tight in the bed of a truck, and the same guy that had been on the hog was coming toward me. They had me positioned on my stomach, but my head was hanging off the bed of the truck. After he tore my anus apart, another did it and then another. Even the guy from school did it." He paused, and when he spoke again his voice was shaky.

"At first I thought I would die. I was hoping I would. I'll never forget that first scream I let out. After a while I just lay there."

Tears began to well up in Donisha's eyes when she saw them streaming down Marcus's face.

"The guy from school never even came back after that, and I never told anyone about it, Donisha. I finished after that semester and came back to Austin." He lifted his head and looked at her. "How can a man say that he was raped? Huh, Donisha? How can a man say that and still be a man?" He wiped his tears away with his hand only to have more fall after them.

"I've questioned my manhood for ten years. I thought that what they did to me made me gay. I didn't want to be that way, but every time a woman turned me down I felt that she knew my secret. I thought that women could see through me and know what happened out there. After a while I just left them both alone, women and men." He looked back up at her.

"When I fell in love with you, I knew I was a man. I was confused before you, but I'm not anymore. At the hospital, that was my first time seeing Terrance in two years. And the only reason he knew I was there is because he works as an orderly there. He had been there when my mother was checked in, and he came back after his shift. He called me after that asking questions about who you were, and I told him. I told him that I love you more than I love myself. I told him that you complete me. I told him that you would be my wife one day. That video has to be more than two years old, because I haven't been with a man or a woman in that long. I wanted to tell you, Donisha. You have to believe me. I know that God used you to show me who I am. I love you, Donisha, I love you with all my heart."

Donisha felt bad for him. She really did, but before her stood a man that had been with other men, and she just couldn't get past that. There was no way that she would ever understand how a man could lay up with another man and claim not to be gay.

When she opened her mouth, all that came out was, "Five minutes is up." She slowly shut the door and went back to her spot on the couch and cried softly.

The next day when Donisha and the kids were at the supermarket, she saw Mr. Black. They made eye contact almost immediately, and within seconds he was headed in her direction.

"Daddy Black, Daddy Black," Ed chanted when he eyed Marcus's father heading their way. Frankie's face lit up and a bright smile appeared on her face when she saw him. Donisha didn't really have anything against Marcus's father, but she was not ready to answer any questions about her relationship with his son.

"Hey, kids," he said excitedly as he picked up Frankie and planted a kiss on her cheek and then turned to Ed and patted him on the head.

"Hello Donisha, how are you doing?" he asked, still holding Frankie but looking at Donisha.

Donisha didn't want to cry in front of him, but she could feel her tears and just when she felt like she was about to burst, he interrupted her.

"I know that relationships go through test and trials as do people, but please don't take the children away from me. With Berta Mae gone, I don't have much to look forward to." He looked at Frankie and continued, "I was reliving my life through their innocent eyes when I was seeing them every day." He looked at Donisha thoughtfully, "I'm an old man now, honey, but sometimes when you snatch the only innocence that a person has left, it tears them apart and it takes a whole lotta God to put em back together again." He swatted his hand gently at Donisha as to dismiss his own words.

"Anyway, honey, I'm just an old man and sometimes I rattle off at the mouth, but I meant what I said. I really love Ed and Frankie, and I would like it if you'd bring them by the house sometimes." He place Frankie back down on her feet and walked close enough to Donisha to wipe away the single tear that slid from her eye.

"I don't meddle in my son's business, but I know for a long time now that something big has been bothering him. I always believed that when it was God's time, I'd find out what it was. I don't know what will happen with you two, but you will always be family to me. And whatever it is that Marcus done, I know he's probably really sorry now. I thank you for everything Donisha, and please don't forget what I said about the kids." He kissed her on the cheek, said his good-byes to the children, and then he was gone. He didn't ask any questions. He just said his peace and was gone.

"Mama, mama, can we go see him?" Ed interrupted her thought process, jumping up and down in front of her like a little jack-in-the-box.

"Yeah, baby," she sighed as she pushed her cart to the front of the store and prepared to checkout. Seeing Marcus's father touched a part of her heart that she thought had died when she learned who Marcus truly was. Marcus came from a good family, so she just couldn't understand why he had been so deceptive and selfish about his past.

Later on that day, Zora called and said that everyone was meeting at The Den and that it was very important that she be there to help with the details for Kyla's wedding. Donisha had been avoiding her friends for weeks. She didn't want them to find out that she had been engaged to a down-low brotha, and she sure didn't feel like trying to explain to them what had happen with the videotape. She knew that she could only avoid them for so long before they figured out that something was wrong. She agreed to meet them at the club at eight o'clock.

Donisha was proud of herself for not going back to the Brown Sugar after Marcus, and she was actually getting used to cleaning up hotel rooms. She knew it wasn't what she wanted to do with her life, but at least she didn't have to sit in the back of the classroom at school hiding from guys that had probably seen her at work. Her mother called shortly after Zora and asked for the kids, which was fine with Donisha since she had made plans with the girls.

Her mother had grown to depend on the kids for companionship since the Bishop had passed away, and Donisha never turned down her mother's need for their company. She knew that her mother was alone now except for her and her siblings. Donisha's brothers and sisters all lived in other cities and states so they weren't as close to their mother as she was.

Donisha packed an overnight bag for the kids and got herself dressed and then dropped them off at her mother's house. By the time she made it to the club, everyone was already there. Donisha could tell that Zora was the happiest to see her and by the look that she kept giving Donisha, she was worried about her. Chelle hugged her tight and kissed her cheek, and Donisha knew that she'd missed her too. Kyla smiled and glowed each time one of the girls mentioned her upcoming wedding, and for the first time in a long time Donisha was truly happy to see Jamie.

Kyla talked about how she didn't want to hire a wedding planner even though Peter and his family could afford it. She said that it had always been her dream to plan her own wedding. They'd formulated a guest list and discussed possible honeymoon spots before Donisha finally asked, "What about sex, Kyla? Can you guys have sex?"

Kyla looked down at her hands before answering and then looked up at Donisha, "Having pleasurable and intimate sex is important in any relationship, guys, and keeping myself and Peter safe and healthy is important too. Oral sex is generally considered to be a low-risk activity, but we will still be able to have regular sex with two or more condoms." She fidgeted around with her hands for a while and then said, "I'm not marrying Peter for sex, though. I love him, and I know that he loves me. I'll be the first to admit that I'm scared as hell, but we'll be smart about sex when we get to it, because we both know all the risks."

Donisha smiled and put her hand on top of Kyla's. "I'm so happy for you, girl. You're the first one of us all that's really found the one."

Kyla looked at her with a puzzled expression, and Donisha excused herself to the restroom. Donisha knew the girls would have questions about the statement she had let slip past her lips. She had announced her engagement to Marcus on the same day that Kyla had announced hers, and now she was singing a different tune.

Zora followed Donisha to the restroom, and Donisha was surprised when Zora caught her wiping her tears. Zora's expression was soft and quizzical.

"What's going on Donisha sweetie?" she asked as she rushed over to the paper towel dispenser.

Donisha responded with loud sniffles and a sigh, "I'm not getting married, Zora."

Zora walked over to Donisha and put her arms around her and hugged her.

"I'm sorry, honey, but if Marcus doesn't want to marry a woman as beautiful as you, then that's his loss." She let Donisha go from their embrace and walked over to the sink so that she could wet the paper towels. "But I thought that he was really the one, Donisha. I mean, he was so good with the kids and he bought you that car." Zora brought the wet paper towels to her friend and began to wipe at her eyes. She wanted to make sure that Zora wouldn't see the tears that were about to fall.

"Zora, I'm so confused. Marcus still wants to marry me, but he did something, which he claims was before we even met, that I just can't seem to get past. I mean, I love him so much, but every time I think about what he did, I feel nothing but utter disgust." Donisha gently took one of the napkins from Zora and wiped at the new tears forming in her eyes.

Zora read her expression with a knowing look on her face and allowed Donisha to continue.

"He was raped by a group of men when he was in college and says that he's been confused about his manhood ever since. He's slept with men before, Zora." The tears began to roll down her cheeks again, but she continued, "He says that the last time was two years ago, and I believe that part, but he says that he isn't confused anymore. He says that he knows now because of me that he is a man. How can I be sure that he's not gay when he's been with a man?"

Zora looked at her and was lost for words. She finally uttered, "Did he have sex with you without telling you that he's been with men, Donisha?" Donisha could tell that Zora was trying to hide the disgust and anger in her voice.

"No," she replied, "Our relationship was never about sex. He never even touched me in that way."

Zora looked away from Donisha as another woman walked into the restroom; and when the stranger saw Donisha's tears, she aborted her mission to use the restroom altogether.

"Donisha, I've never been put in the situation that you are in, so I can't tell you what I would do. It is possible that he was confused after being raped, and it is also possible that he is straight now. But I agree that it would be hard to be with a man who used to be with men. Women have come to a place where we can combine the separate spheres and cross over from the original American ideals of what roles women are supposed to hold. But this is still a gray area for men. God is the one you need to be talking to. Cause if you love this man like I think you do, then your heart needs resolution."

Donisha nodded her head and hugged Zora before saying, "Please just let this be between us. I don't want the others to know. It's just so embarrassing." Zora nodded her head at her friend, understanding her position, and they both left the bathroom.

When they returned to the table, Donisha began to listen to the conversation that the other girls were already having. Chelle told them about the girl that was living with her and how her ex-boyfriend Ty had gotten the fourteen-year-old girl pregnant. She told them about how the girl's mother and her boyfriend had locked her up and abused her and how she'd escaped.

Donisha was amazed at how Chelle's life had changed within a matter of months. Mia was living with her now, and Chelle was going to court after the baby was born to obtain permanent guardianship rights for Mia. Chelle told them about Mia not wanting the baby and how she planned to give the baby up for adoption. Donisha felt bad for the unborn child when she thought about how she'd done Frankie, but she knew that a fourteen year old could not possibly raise a baby. At least Mia had a valid reason for not wanting to raise her child. Donisha had never been able to come up with a real reason for giving up Frankie.

Donisha could see the excitement in Zora's eyes as she talked about Emory, his job, and how just by watching his passion for his work had changed her life. Donisha also noticed Zora's slight obsession with Mia and wondered if it was healthy for her. Donisha had always felt bad about Zora losing her baby and not being able to have children again.

They all knew about how Zora felt that Bryan was to blame for her inability to have children. So, they were surprised by her revealing that he had come by and given her the opportunity to forgive him. Donisha was proud of the woman that Zora was becoming and could see change in everyone except for Jamie as they sat around the table and updated each other on their lives.

After her night with the girls, Donisha felt good. She had finally been able to release some of the accumulated pain that she was feeling about Marcus when she talked to Zora.

The house was quiet with the kids at her mother's, and even though it was late she plopped down on the couch and turned on the television. She flipped through the channels until she came to BET. While the commercials played, she looked up toward the ceiling and felt her eyes become watery.

"Lord," she began, "I need you now. Please show me which way I need to go. I know that you can do all things and if this man that I love is truly healed, Lord, you let me know." She wiped the tears from her eyes and looked toward the television. The lady that was speaking was wearing a beautiful, two piece, cream-colored suit. Her raspy voice sounded as if she were squeezing out the words.

"Stay tuned for an encore presentation of *The Donnie McClurkin Story: From Darkness to Light.*" Donisha had heard of Donnie McClurkin. Her mother and even Marcus had his CDs. Donisha liked the man's voice and when she heard the lyrics playing at her mother's house or in Marcus's car, she could feel the anointing in them. She decided that she would stay up and watch the program so that she could know more about the powerful voice that she had admired in the past.

ZORA

§

That Sunday, church was good. Zora and Emory rode together, and she thought that she would feel down because right after church was over, she was supposed to take him to the airport. She didn't feel down at all though. There was a happiness that had resided in her since she'd opened her eyes that morning. She knew that Emory was leaving, but more than that, she felt in her heart that her friend was coming back just as he had before.

Zora saw Chelle and Mia come into the sanctuary shortly after she and Emory took their seats. She wondered why they didn't sit in the two seats that she had saved for them beside her, but her questions were answered later on in the service when Royce came in and sat down next to Chelle. She winked at Chelle, and Chelle smiled back at her. Donisha, her mother, and her children were already sitting in the row in front of Zora when she took her seat, and she was so happy to see that her friend had found the strength to come to church. They looked good. Donisha's mother was always sharp in her expensive, classy suits, but today she was wearing the mess out of a white suit and matching hat.

Donisha even looked chic in her tailored pantsuit. Zora smiled, thinking about how Donisha used to dress when she did come to church in the past; her clothes had been so skin-tight that they left nothing to the imagination. Frankie looked adorable with her signature ponytails and her cute flowery spring dress, and Ed was equally handsome in his dressy slacks and collared shirt.

Zora could see Jamie in the front row, and Kyla and Peter sat right behind her.

The service was different that day. The pastor said that God had dropped in his spirit step out of tradition and let the spirit lead. The congregation stood and began to give God praise, and the pastor stepped his stout, robe-covered body out of the pulpit and walked down the middle aisle. Zora was surprised when the pastor stopped at her row and pointed his finger at her.

"Child come, the Lord's got a word for you." Emory stepped aside and let Zora out into the aisle. The pastor put his hand on her head and two of the ushers came up behind her and stood as spotters. Zora didn't know what they were expecting, but she closed her eyes and listened as the pastor spoke.

"He says he knows that your womb has been painful to your heart. He has listened to your cries. Eliokum shabbaha." Zora knew that Pastor Leo was speaking in tongues, but she didn't know where the river of tears came from. He was right. The idea of never being able to bear children was beginning to wear on her, but how did he know?

"He says everything is working out for your children's sake." Zora's eyes shot open. She knew that he was making a mistake. Maybe he had called the wrong person into the aisle, or maybe he wasn't even a true man of God, but she allowed him to continue anyway.

"He is blessing your womb," he said as he placed the hand that wasn't on her head on her stomach. "He says your new job is to be a mother. He says he's about to perform a miracle in your life."

That was the last thing that Zora heard before she passed out. She thought that she had felt something special, but she wasn't sure. The pastor had spoke things into her life that were beyond impossible. When she came to, she thought that maybe the mere hypocrisy of the pastor's words had made her to pass out.

By the time the ushers finally got her up with Emory's help and guided her back to her seat the pastor, had one of his hands on a young girl's head and the other on her stomach.

Zora could only think to herself, "Good, he found the right person." She stood and listened along with the rest of the church as the pastor ministered to the child.

"This baby in your womb is his will. It was conceived out of sin, but he will be born pleasing to God. Dear child," he continued. Zora could tell that the pastor was now crying, and she really wished that she could get close enough to see the girl's face.

"God says everything you've asked him for is already done. He says he has a special place for you, a special job for you. He says the answer to your question is "yes dear child, yes." Eli hababa shokum, eli hababa!" When the girl fell backwards, Zora almost did too. It was Mia. The pastor had been ministering to Mia.

After Mia hit the floor and the ushers and Chelle surrounded her, the pastor went further to the back of the church. "Come here, son," Zora heard him say. Zora turned around to see who he was talking to, and there stood Marcus. She looked to the row in front of her and saw Donisha standing with tears running down her face. When she looked back at Marcus, his face was covered with tears. He held his hand up and awaited the pastor's words.

"Eliokum shabablikom," the pastor screamed in his face, "God says that the things you have been through and done were not for you, son." He began to speak in tongues again, and Zora felt that Marcus's experience with the pastor was far more intense than hers or Mia's.

"It took a certain kind of strength for you to walk that walk without taking yourself out. He says you kept on asking, "Why me?" Zora saw Marcus's tall frame bend slightly, and his hands dropped to clutch his stomach as he cried out thank you.

The pastor went on, "He says he chose you. It had to be you. He knew that you were strong enough. He chose you to carry thousands of confused men on your back."

The pastor went on speaking in tongues, "It's time son. It's time to tell it. He brought you out, now tell it." With those words Marcus hit the floor the same way Zora and Mia had. After Marcus, Zora heard the pastor speak into the lives of others, but none that she knew.

She missed Emory as soon as she dropped him off at the airport later on that day, but she understood his mission now. Even though she knew he would really be gone a whole month this time, she'd watched him go with a smile and told him to be safe. She'd even felt the excitement of how his being there could actually change and save lives. She thought about the stories that he had shared about his first trip before he had left. He had told her about a time when the convoy he was traveling with was robbed for their provisions by an army of rebel boys.

"Babies," he had said shaking his head sadly. "'Donnez-moi la nourriture (Give me the food),' is all the kid said to me," he sighed.

"I will be blessed to save a few of these kids. They are born with no chance. They fight AIDS in the womb, and then once they are born, and they fight the raping and ravaging of their land and their bodies."

"I met this one kid at the camp," Emory was smiling now, "he was doing anything to capture my attention. They call him KiKo. He has the biggest, saddest eyes in the world to me. He was offering to tote water, food, and supplies for me. I asked Roy what was going on with the little dude, and Roy told me that he was offering his services to me in hopes that I would bring him home as my slave." They sat quietly for a while, and then Emory spoke again, "I wish I could save them all."

They had prayed together before he left. They had asked God to protect them both as they journeyed through life.

After their prayer, Zora was sure Emory would find her waiting for him in a month.

She wished she had the courage to go, and of course Emory had asked, but at that point Zora knew that she was need in America. Mia needed her and more than that she needed Mia.

It was Sunday night, and she knew that Chelle would drop Mia off the next morning. She looked forward to their time together and had planned on taking her to the zoo the next day. She knew that she coddled Mia as if she was a small child, but she thought that a child as mistreated as her deserved special treatment. She was excited about the next day as she prepared her dinner for one of shrimp scampi and pasta.

When the phone rang, she became excited. Even though she wanted it to be Emory saying he was at the airport waiting for her, deep down she knew it wasn't.

"Hello?" she answered.

"Hey Zora," Chelle almost chanted, "I need the biggest favor from you tonight."

Zora sighed jokingly, "What do you want now ole worrisome gal?"

Zora and Chelle shared a laugh before Chelle continued, "Well Royce just called and invited me to a play, and I wanted to know if we could drop Mia off there. You know how I worry about her, and I don't want to leave her here alone."

Zora replied in a more serious tone, "Yeah, sure Chelle. You know I'll do anything for you and her. Why don't you just let her stay the night so you don't have to come back in the morning?"

"Are you sure, Zora? I know Em's gone, but you're already doing so much for us."

Zora put her hand on her hip and even though Chelle couldn't see her, she took a motherly stance and said, "Could you please hurry up and bring that girl over here Chelle?"

Zora thought she heard tears in Chelle's voice when she said, "I don't know what I'd do without you."

By the time Mia arrived, Zora had been to the video store and back. She had rented *Princess Diaries 2* and the remake of *Freaky Friday* with Jamie Lee Curtis and Lindsay Lohan. She popped popcorn and made sure that the bedroom that was hers as a child was clean enough for her guest.

Zora knew that the bedroom hadn't been touched in twelve years, but she wanted to check anyway. The last time she even opened the door was the day that she moved back into her parents' house after they died. When she opened the door, she was flooded with memories. The huge white wooden canopy bed still sat in the middle of the room, and the pink plushy carpet and walls almost swallowed Zora and her chestnut skin in her burgundy silk pajamas. She remembered her thirteenth birthday and how her mother and father had closed her eyes as she walked down the hall to the bedroom. She had been so surprised to see all the plaques that plastered the walls with phrases like *Girls Rule* and *100% Girl.* Her biggest joy had been the bookshelves that they had built into one of the walls. It took her the rest of her middle-school years and all of her high-school years to fill it with novels, books of poetry, and African American art books. Her parents had been so proud when she'd squeezed the last book in there.

That was the day they told her that she had been their last chance to have a child. Her mother had endometriosis, and they thought that they had waited too late to conceive. Finally after ten years of trying and failing, Zora had been born. She felt tears sting her eyes as she closed the door and thought to herself, "Mia will love that room."

She had been right too; Mia loved the room. She and Zora sat on the bed while Zora told her about her memories that had taken place in the room. She told Mia about how her parents had presented her with the room when they redecorated it; in fact, she filled the child in on her life up when she had left it for college. Zora eyed Mia peculiarly.

"Mia, sweetie, what do you want to be when you grow up?" Zora asked as if the thought to question Mia's future had just occurred to her.

Mia looked back at Zora thoughtfully and smiled, "God has a special place for me, and I don't know what it is yet, but I'm looking forward to it."

Zora smiled sweetly and said, "I think that you'll make a really good teacher one day. It helps to know things about life to be able to teach others. In fact that's really what life is. Teaching others." Zora stroked Mia's tiny braids. "Whatever you become, I'll be proud of you. You are such a beautiful girl with so much to look forward to in life."

Mia's smile disappeared, "What about the baby? Did the pastor really mean that God thinks it's special?"

Zora looked at Mia's protruding belly and sighed. Mia was six months pregnant, and this was the first time that she had ever mentioned the child growing inside her. Zora knew from experience that at her stage in the pregnancy some sort of attachment had to be forming. "Mia, I think this baby will be very special. You are special, and anything that is a part of you has to be too." Mia nodded her head and smiled again.

The next day Zora carried out her plans by taking Mia to the zoo. Mia was like a kid in a candy store. She had never been to the zoo and was intrigued by all the animals they saw. As much fun as she was having, after a while Mia's legs began to hurt, and she started to complain about stomach cramps. When they left the zoo, Zora stopped by Zapeta's so that they could eat lunch. Mia ate a lot, and every time she'd belch she would place her hand on her stomach and laugh.

"It's kicking, and it feels so funny. I still haven't got used to it," she finally said letting Zora in on the joke.

Zora looked over the table as Mia grabbed her hand and moved it over the table to her stomach. Zora laughed when the baby kicked her hand and felt so proud that Mia was finally acknowledging the baby. She couldn't wait to tell Chelle.

CHELLE

§

Mia had been complaining about stomach cramps for a few days, and it had started bothering Chelle. She called Zora and told her that she was taking the child to the doctor that day instead of bringing her to Zora's house. Zora was OK with it but still asked if Mia was OK. Chelle assured Zora that Mia was fine and told her that she just needed to find out why her stomach was cramping.

Chelle had noticed that Mia was a lot more talkative and even brought up the baby often while they conversed.

"What was your Aunt Mattie like?" Mia asked Chelle in the car as they rode to the clinic. A huge smile spread across Chelle's face. Even though she had told Mia about her aunt before, she had no problem with telling her about her again. She liked talking about her aunt. For Chelle, talking about her Aunt Mattie kept her spirit alive.

"Well, she was a strong black woman. She gave me so much in the little time that I had with her. I moved here to be near her. She offered me what my parents didn't, and that was a family." Chelle smiled harder and said, "Her smile alone could bust open the heavens. She loved so hard. I've never known a person quite like her, and I probably won't know another Aunt Mattie."

Mia laid her head back in the seat and smiled as Chelle pulled into a parking space at the clinic. Chelle's phone rang just as she and Mia were about to get out of the car.

"Hello," she answered, knowing that the number that showed up on the caller ID was her mother's. She had been waiting for her mother to call so that she could tell her what was going on in her life, but now she felt nervous.

"Hello dear," her mother replied in her usual cheery voice, "How are you?"

"I'm fine, mother," she replied while instructing Mia with a wave of her hand to get out of the car as she did the same. "How are you and daddy?"

"We're as good as ever," her mother lied. "We were just looking over bank statements this morning and noticed how you were going through you monthly allowance faster these days. Is everything OK? How is the new place?"

Chelle exhaled as she began to tell her mother about Ty and how she had come to know Mia. She told her about how her allowance wasn't just for her anymore, but she was sure to let her know that her status hadn't changed regarding her school standing. By the time the doctor called Mia into his office, Chelle was awaiting her mother's scolding voice. Chelle put her on hold and told the doctor to go ahead and begin the examination, and she would be back as soon as her phone call ended. When she put her ear back to the phone and said hello, she heard her mother's voice.

"I have always questioned your ability to make decisions as an adult, Rachelle. You've made terrible decisions based on your emotions. The decision to move to Austin in the first place always puzzled me. The law schools in New York are much more prestigious than any in the South. Now though, Rachelle, I see you are a responsible young woman. As long as you remain in school, then your father and I will support you. We will put an extra five hundred dollars in your account each month. We will try to make it there to meet the child as soon as possible."

Chelle was surprised but happy to have her mother's support and as soon as she hung up the phone, she went to the examination room where Mia and the doctor were. When Dr. Kuo was done with the examination, she asked Mia to get dressed and told Chelle to follow her into her office.

"Well," she began, "Mia has been through a very traumatic experience. I'm not sure if the leaking is coming from stress or from her young age, but Mia will not carry this baby to term. Her amniotic sac has a small hole in it and is leaking most of the fluids that the baby needs to survive. Her cramps are actually contractions, and although she's only dilated half a centimeter, I want to have her admitted into the hospital until it's time for the baby to be born."

"Is Mia gonna be OK?" Chelle asked in a warbly, worried tone.

The doctor nodded her head, "Mia's fine at this point. The baby is fighting a bigger battle than Mia. Mia is close to her thirtieth week of pregnancy, but it's still too early for the baby to be born. I gave her a shot to help the baby's lungs develop faster, and I also gave her something for the baby's muscles, but at this point we'll just have to wait and see what happens."

Chelle nodded her head at the doctor and replied, "Please do whatever you can."

Chelle sat in the waiting area of the clinic, waiting for the ambulance to come and get Mia. She called Zora and Royce and filled them in on what was going on. Zora promised to come to the hospital as soon as Chelle called and let her know that Mia was settled in a hospital room. Royce told Chelle that he would be there as soon as his shift was over.

Many thoughts raced through Chelle's head, but the biggest worry that plagued her was the thought that the unwanted baby would die. Mia hadn't wanted the baby at all before that day at church, and now the baby would probably die. Chelle felt ashamed of all the times that she had ignored Mia's protruding belly and went along with the act that the baby didn't exist. She said a silent prayer for the unborn child and followed the ambulance to the hospital.

Once Mia was settled in a room, Chelle called Zora. While they waited for Zora's arrival, Chelle and Mia watched an old rerun of *Family Matters.* They were both looking at the television, but not really watching the show. Mia finally spoke up.

"Do you think the baby will die?" Her voice held the curiosity of a child's, and Chelle was tempted to sugarcoat her answer as an adult would do for a child.

Chelle reached over and stroked Mia's hair as she answered, "I don't know, sweetie. The doctors will do all they can for the baby, but we really have to wait and see."

Tears began to fill the child's eyes. "I thought that I didn't want the baby, but I don't want it to die. If the baby dies then what does that mean about God? He said that the baby would be special. What does it mean if the baby dies?"

Chelle looked at Mia with sympathetic eyes, "Mia, this baby is special whether it lives or dies. God has a plan for everyone, and we both have to trust in his plan. We may not understand it sweetie, but we don't have to. It's still his perfect plan without our understanding."

When Zora arrived, she had a big balloon bouquet and flowers for Mia. She sat down in the other chair next to the bed and grabbed Mia's hand. They all sat in silence while the television watched them and they explored their own thoughts.

When Royce tapped softly on the door they all looked to see who would come from the other side. They thought it was one of the nurses coming in to check on Mia and were surprised to see Royce walk into the room with an oversized stuffed panda bear with a card attached to his chest. Chelle smiled a real smile for the first time that day and got up to go and greet her friend.

He whispered loud enough for everyone to hear. "How is she doing?" Mia smiled at Royce. She had come to appreciate his relationship with Chelle. She loved Chelle, which meant that she loved to see her happy. Whenever Royce was around, Chelle seemed to be worry-free and smiled a lot more than she did when he wasn't. In her young mind, Mia knew that she made Chelle happy, but she also knew that Royce offered up completeness that she wasn't equipped to give.

"I'm fine, Mr. Royce," she said, "You don't have to whisper."

They all laughed, which lifted the thickness from the room. Mia loved the panda and insisted that it sit at the foot of her hospital bed. Royce asked Zora and Chelle if they were hungry, and Zora insisted that Chelle go with Royce on his proposed food run to get some fresh air.

After Chelle's initial refusal to leave Mia's side, Chelle finally left the hospital with Royce and they drove to the same deli that she had taken Mia to on the first day they had met. As they waited at the counter for the four sandwiches and three soups that they had ordered, Royce stared at Chelle pensively. Chelle didn't grow nervous under his stare but curious.

"What?" she asked with a shy smile. Royce grinned and grasped her hand.

"Every day you grow more wonderful, Chelle. You have a good heart, and I'm glad that Tyrone character couldn't see it." He laughed at his owned thoughts and continued, "I'm even kind of glad that he hit you. If it hadn't been for that I wouldn't have ever met you. As bad as it may sound, if he hadn't done what he did to Mia, she may not have been saved." Chelle watched emotion overtake Royce's face.

"When I was five years old, my father beat my mother to death over a ten dollar vial of crack and then turned around and shot himself in the head right in front of me. That day when I went to Mia's house, so many memories hit me. I came back to the hospital, because I saw something in you at your house that day with Tyrone. You didn't have to tell us about the girl, but you did. I knew that you would take her. God blessed me with good foster parents, but I knew with Mia being so old and pregnant that not too many people would have been willing to take on that burden." A smile returned to Royce's face, and he said, "Mia and I are both lucky to have you."

Chelle stood up on her tiptoes, and Royce leaned down and they shared their first kiss—a beautiful kiss.

When they got back to the hospital room, there were two nurses and a doctor standing over Mia's bed while Zora stood back with a worried look on her face.

"What's going on?" Chelle asked with apprehension in her voice.

"We are going to have to go ahead and induce her labor, ma'am," the doctor said turning to Chelle. "She's dilated a whole centimeter, so we're just going to go ahead and speed up the process."

"But I thought the baby wasn't ready," Chelle said in a panicked tone.

"Well, the baby is underdeveloped and may suffer a few problems once he gets here, but Mia is having a few problems herself. She is bleeding severely, and that is posing a threat. We've spoken with Dr. Kuo, and she is on her way. She will be here to deliver the baby."

Chelle nodded her head, almost oblivious to the fact that she was nodding. Zora reached out and placed her hand on one of Chelle shoulders, and Royce placed his hand on the other shoulder as they guided her out into the hall while the nurses and doctors hurried to prepare the room for the birth of the premature child.

DONISHA

§

Donisha moved throughout the kitchen as if it was hers. Mrs. Black had kept all of her cooking utensils in very predictable places. It was the middle of the week, and she was cooking chicken and dressing, greens, yams, and baked beans.

She could hear Mr. Black and the children talking and playing in the den, and she smiled a real smile for the first time in weeks. The program she had watched on BET about Donnie McClurkin last week and the service at church the following day had somehow changed her life.

Mr. McClurkin's life had been so different from Marcus's, but it had been easy for Donisha to relate his story to Marcus's. He had suffered rape through most of his adolescence and had felt the same feelings of confusion that Marcus had described. Donisha had cried throughout the whole program. Mr. McClurkin said that people from his past were trying to come up against him, and Donisha thought of Terrance. The best part of the program was to see that God had brought this man through all his confusion and pain for a purpose. The pain and hurt had been for others, and Mr. McClurkin wasn't ashamed of what happened to him as long as his story benefited others that were suffering rape or confusion. She found herself thanking God for allowing her to see the program and thought that Marcus needed to see it too. It was just her luck that three days later it aired again and she recorded it.

She had called Mr. Black at the beginning of the week and told him that she wanted to cook dinner on Wednesday at his house. She told him to invite Marcus over but not to tell him that she would be there. She had even invited her mother. She'd heard everything that Pastor Leo had said to Marcus and wanted to help him in any way that she could. After dinner, she wanted them all to sit down and watch the video of Donnie McClurkin, and she knew that God would lead the rest of the evening.

Mr. Black had told Donisha that he hadn't really seen too much of his son, but he was sure that he would come when he called.

Donisha was almost done with dinner when the doorbell rang. She saw Mr. Black pass the kitchen and glide to the front door. She felt butterflies in her stomach and knew she was nervous when she felt her hands begin to sweat.

"Oh my," Mr. Black exclaimed in a loud voice, "It's not every day that a beautiful woman shows up on my porch. How can I help you?"

Donisha hit her forehead with the palm of her hand. She'd forgotten to tell him that her mother would be coming. She rushed out of the kitchen to the front door to explain and was surprised to find her mother with a wide smile across her face. Mr. Black was as handsome a man as Marcus, but Donisha never expected her mother to notice. Her mother did indeed look beautiful. This was the first time since her father's death that Donisha had seen her without her signature housedress on outside of Sundays. Her mother was a short, stout woman with milk chocolate skin and high cheekbones. Donisha was the spitting image of her, no doubt.

"I'm sorry, Mr. Black. I forgot to tell you that mama was coming." The kids were now charging the door and chanting, "Granny, granny."

"Oh, nonsense Donisha. No sorry necessary. Your mother is as welcome here as you and the kids." He took her mother's hand and guided her into the den where he had been entertaining the kids. Donisha stood at the door and shook her head as she grinned at his flirtatious antics. As she was about to walk back into the kitchen, she heard the screen door shut and when she turned around she smiled warmly.

Marcus stood there with an uneasy look on his face. It was as if he was afraid of what she would say or do, and she immediately felt bad for all of the hurtful names that she had called him.

She walked toward him and opened her arms, greeting him with a much needed embrace. He pushed her away from him with questions on his face. Donisha knew he was wondering why she was being so friendly after weeks of ignoring him.

"I understand, Marcus. I finally understand. I want to be here for you if you'll still have me."

Marcus looked at her in awe. Confusion melted away from his face, and relief replaced it. "I'm so sorry for how I hurt you Donisha, but I love you so much. Of course I'll still have you."

Donisha called out to Ed and Frankie and when they came down the hallway and saw Marcus, they both screamed and ran toward him. It seemed like they stood there and embraced for hours, and for the first time ever Donisha felt like she had a family of her own.

Donisha blushed hard when everyone commented on how good her meal was. Even the kids had cleaned their plates. Mr. Black was in the family room teaching Mrs. Raines how to play chess, and the kids were on the floor in front of the television coloring in giant-sized books.

Marcus was helping Donisha with the dishes when she said, "Could you please go into the den and get everyone ready to watch something? I brought a video, and I want us all to sit and watch it as a family." Marcus smiled brightly as he headed into the family room. Donisha hoped that she was doing the right thing by showing everyone the video. She knew Marcus would need his family's support while he went through this, and she thought that this video would help them to understand what he went through.

When she finished in the kitchen and walked into the den, everyone was sitting and waiting like small children eager for candy. Donisha told Ed and Frankie that they could go into the kitchen and finish coloring. They were happy to oblige, and Donisha went ahead and put the videotape into the VCR.

Donisha watched Marcus throughout the program, and the tears never stopped falling from his eyes. She heard her mother say "Glory be to God," a few times, and Mr. Black would even say "That's all right, now," as Donnie McClurkin told his story. When the program ended and the credits started rolling, Mr. Black looked over at Donisha and said, "That was a pretty good program. I been listening to that young man's music for quite a while now, and I never knew that his glory came from that kind of story."

When she looked at him to reply, Marcus was standing in front of the TV. They all looked up at him, and it was only then that Mr. Black and Mrs. Raines noticed his tears.

"Daddy, there's something that I've held in for so long, and I can't hold it in anymore."

He looked over at Donisha and smiled through his tears. "I told you God used you, didn't I? Baby, I want you to know that I never would have been able to do this without you." Donisha smiled as Marcus began to tell his story and knew that she had done the right thing.

Marcus followed Donisha home after dinner so that they could put the children to bed and talk. Marcus's father had surprised them with his tears, but he said that he was proud of his son for choosing to tell his story. Mrs. Raines had tilted her head at her daughter and smiled. "Girl, God gave you the tools to soften the blow." They listened attentively as Marcus explained to them that this would not be the last time that he told his story.

Marcus had to help her get the kids out of the truck, because they had both fallen asleep. Marcus carried Ed's long body, and Donisha cradled Frankie as if she were an infant. As soon as they were inside Donisha's apartment, Frankie lifted her head.

"Mommy Nisha," she said in a groggy voice, "Where is my picture I drew at Daddy Black's?" Donisha looked around for Marcus who had all the kids' pictures in his hand, while cradling Ed's sleeping body in his arms.

"Wait a second. Let me put your brother down, and I'll give it to you," Marcus told her.

Frankie climbed down from her mother's arms and walked over to where Marcus was gently laying Ed down on the couch. Marcus handed her the pictures, and she began to rummage through them like she was looking for something in particular. She walked back over to where her mother stood.

"Here," she said, handing her mother the paper that she had fished out of the pile.

Donisha looked at the paper and then back down at Frankie who was rubbing her eyes sleepily. "Who is it sweetie?" Donisha could tell that she had drawn a picture of a man, but she couldn't tell who he was. It was a tall stick figure with a big chest that puffed out with pride.

Frankie smiled as she turned to go down the hall to the bedroom that she shared with her brother. "That's grandpa, but he looks different because his chest is poking out. It was poking out when I saw him in my dream in the car too. But he said he's all right, he's just so proud of you."

Donisha looked over at Marcus with big tears in her eyes, and his open arms told her that there would always be a smile and a hug waiting for her with him.

ZORA

§

Zora stood in the waiting room along with Chelle and Royce and was just as worried about Mia and the baby as they were. She knew deep down inside that Mia had become attached to the child that she was carrying. She knew that the death of this baby would break Mia's spirit, and she sure didn't want to see the child more broken than she already was.

Chelle paced the floor while Royce looked up at the television. Zora watched from a corner of the room where she stood against the wall. She wished so bad that Emory was there with her.

When Dr. Kuo emerged from the room, she beckoned for Chelle to come over to her, and Zora and Royce rushed over right behind her. "Mia is dilating rapidly, and the baby is not as small as we thought," she said, "In fact, there are no signs indicating that he will not make it." Dr. Kuo looked at Chelle with a serious face, "She's almost reached full dilation and two of you can be present when she delivers the baby. I just need you guys to figure out who it will be and get scrubbed up. By the time you're done we should be ready."

Dr. Kuo disappeared back into the room, and Royce gave Zora a gentle nudge forward.

"You go. Just stick your head out after the baby is born and let me know everything's all right." Zora smiled at him and followed Chelle to the nurses' station to find out where they were supposed to go and scrub up.

By the time Zora and Chelle entered the room, Dr. Kuo had Mia's legs up in stir-ups. They walked over to the end over the bed where Mia lay with a big smile on her face.

"Hey sweetie," Chelle said with a smile that was equally as big. "Are you all right?"

"The doctor says that it's almost over. She said that she's gonna tell me when to push and then the baby will slide out." Her face became serious but still held evidence of happiness.

"I want to see my baby, Chelle. I don't want to throw it away. I want him to be happy. Please make him happy, Chelle. I want you to take him."

Chelle's eyes widened as she looked at Zora and then back at Mia. "Of course, sweetie. Whatever you want. We can keep him." Zora felt tears well up in her eyes as she watched them in silence.

"No Chelle, I want you to keep him. I can't do it, but I know you can." Chelle nodded her head and turned to the doctor when she yelled for Mia to push.

Chelle grabbed Mia's hand as she squeezed hers and pushed with all her might. Dr. Kuo kept telling her that she was doing a good job and that she was almost there.

She pushed three more times before the little boy slid out into the world. Chelle kept hold of Mia's hand as Zora ran over to where the nurses were cleaning and weighing the crying baby.

Dr. Kuo still sat on a stool between Mia's legs, and Chelle heard panic in her voice when she told the nurse, "She's hemorrhaging." Chelle looked at Mia's face, and it was a sea of calmness. Chelle began to rub her hand and tell her how proud she was when Mia cut her off.

"I wish that I could be Aunt Mattie next time, so that I could give you back all the things that you gave me." Chelle looked up and saw the worried expression on Zora's face and how all the nurses were hurrying around the room. Two more doctors joined Dr. Kuo at the other end of the bed when she yelled "code blue" and one nurse was headed toward Mia and Chelle with the tiny baby in her arms and Zora on her heels. She bent over and gently laid the baby on Mia's chest. Mia looked down at him with tears in her eyes.

"All I have to give is him. He can be your family. Please take him. Love him like you love me, and I'll love you back through his heart."

Chelle and Zora were no longer paying attention to the doctors and nurses that were working hard to stop Mia's bleeding. They didn't hear Dr. Kuo when she shouted out, "We're losing her!"

They were both entranced by Mia's voice as she spoke to them, "Name him Matthew, but please call him Mattie." Chelle picked up the baby from Mia's chest and held him in her arms. Mia looked at both Zora and Chelle and smiled. "Remember that special place that God said he had for me? I'm going now, and I'm not even scared." A tear fell from her eye and she continued, "I love you, and please tell Emory that I know God loves me, because I'm here." Zora and Chelle's silent tears became loud cries when Mia closed her eyes, and one of the doctors said in a defeated but familiar tone, "We lost her. Call the time."

Zora had wanted to stay with Mia's lifeless body until the people from the morgue came to take her away, but the doctors only gave her a few more minutes with Mia. Chelle had left the room with Royce to go into the waiting area and speak with the people that were coming to take Mia's body to the funeral home.

As Zora looked at the body that used to bear Mia's spirit she couldn't understand how God could take her away. She was such an innocent child and had been through so much in life. She longed to question him about his plan, but she couldn't forget her words to Mia just a few hours earlier, "We may not understand it, sweetie, but we don't have to. It's still his perfect plan, even without our understanding."

Zora couldn't stop crying, and when she came out of the room she was surprised to see Marcus and Donisha coming toward her. Donisha held Zora and stroked her back as she whispered, "I know, baby, let it out." Donisha's comforting embrace only made her cry harder, but Donisha kept talking, "Sometimes we don't understand things, but God knows best. She can't hurt anymore, Zora. Her pain is over."

Zora had heard those same words the day her mother and father died. Countless people had whispered them to her for comfort, but this time she actually heard them. Mia had lived a rough and unfair life. As much as Zora wanted to spoil her and hated to see her go, she knew that she could never fix that child's past. God did have a special place for her, and it was with him.

CHELLE

§

Chelle couldn't believe that Mia was gone. In such a short time she had become Chelle's life, and now that she was gone she didn't know what she would do with the rest of it. Chelle hadn't spent the night in her apartment since Mia's death. She had spent endless hours at the hospital with Mattie, and then she would go to Zora's. Zora hadn't seen Mattie since the day that Mia died, so Chelle kept her informed on his development. He was a beautiful baby. He had Mia's caramel skin, but Chelle hadn't been able to see his cat-gray eyes until his third day of life. The child had struggled in the beginning. His eyes were covered to protect him from the phototherapy lights that were helping with the slight jaundice. Mattie had been a fighter, though. He was doing fine by day three. His hair was thin and straight, and he had a hairy little body. His tiny fingers and toes always made Chelle smile.

Donisha, Kyla, and Jamie had all been great. They knew that Zora and Chelle were both grieving, and they came through as true friends to help during the process. Even Royce had been at the hospital and Zora's house every day.

By the time of the funeral four days later, accepting that Mia was gone had become a little easier for them. The service was a small but nice graveside service, and it made Chelle sad to see that she and her friends were all Mia ever really had. Pastor Leo had said something that would forever keep Chelle at peace with Mia's death, and as Chelle thought about it she couldn't help but smile.

"Children," he spoke in an authoritative voice, "the Bible says that to be absent from the body is to be present with the Lord." He smiled out at the audience of Mia's new family as they sat in chairs in front of the casket. "She made it home. God has a time and a place for us all, and her time is now and her place is with the lord."

After the service, she and Zora decided to go back to Chelle's place and pack up Mia's room and get it ready for the baby.

Mattie had entered the world weighing only four pounds, two ounces, but the doctors were already saying that he could come home as soon as he could suckle a bottle's nipple. Since Chelle had temporary custody of Mia, it was easy for her to get the adoption paperwork started for Matthew Milan Carter. Chelle had already signed his birth certificate and given him his mother's last name. She decided that he would always know her.

As they packed up the room, they spilled their silent tears over everything they touched. Zora cleaned out the closet and boxed up all of the maternity clothes that Mia had accumulated while living with Chelle. She cleaned out the drawers and boxed up Mia's personal clothes. By the time they finished with the room, the only thing that hadn't been touched was the sign that Zora had bought Mia. They stood in the door, and as they looked up at the sign that read *I Live Here,* tears fell and they embraced each other because they knew that Mia really did live there.

After they were done, they left the apartment and headed to the hospital. Chelle had asked Zora to drop her off so that she could spend some time with Mattie. Royce was already there waiting by the neonatal nursery door with his daddy bracelet on his wrist. One of the doctors had seen him there the whole time, and since Zora had been reluctant about getting close to the baby, Chelle offered the bracelet to him.

She smiled when she saw him and fell into his warm embrace. As they washed their hands in the big hall basin that the doctors, nurses, and visiting parents used for sterilizing their hands before touching the babies, he smiled and said, "I have a surprise for you."

She smiled back at him and asked, "What is it?"

"You'll see," he said as he led her into the nursery.

When Chelle saw Mattie's crib, she was surprised. The day before when she left, he had a tube running from his nose to a syringe that was full of infant formula. He had an IV in his tiny foot and heart monitors all over his tiny body.

The tube was gone this time, and he only had one heart monitor on his chest.

"I think he'll be coming home with you soon, Chelle. The doctor said that you will have to stay overnight on his last night, but I think you guys will be leaving this place real soon," Royce said. "Can you give me your keys, so that I can go and take care of a few things for you?"

Chelle handed him her keys and bent over the crib so that she could hold Mattie in her arms. She sat and sang to the baby and visited with the other new parents that came in to visit their sick or small children for three hours before Royce returned and dropped her keys in her hand.

"So are you going back to Zora's tonight?" he asked as he gently brushed his lips across Mattie's forehead.

"I think I'll get you to take me home." Chelle knew that she surprised him when she asked, "Do you think you can stay with me?"

"Yes," he smiled, "Let's let this little man sleep and get outta here."

Chelle and Royce stopped by a burger stand and grabbed something to eat, and she could feel herself grow eager to live in her own home again.

When she entered the living room, it was dark and she flipped on the light. Royce walked in past her and sat the food down on the coffee table. She walked toward the back of the apartment and stopped at the door that she and Zora had shut only a few hours earlier. She twisted the knob, and when the door opened her eyes flooded with tears.

In the center of the room sat a big brown, round crib decorated in denim bedding. A mobile with brown teddy bears wearing denim overalls hung above the crib. When she shifted her eyes from the bed, she saw the blue border that ran around the whole length of the walls. Above the border on one of the walls were giant letters that spelled: MATTIE. But what really touched her heart was the sign that Zora had bought for Mia.

Zora had felt that Mia needed pictures of herself around the house to feel at home and took a simple snapshot of her sitting on the porch at her house. She had framed the picture and given it to Chelle who had put it on the coffee table.

Royce had had the picture blown up to poster size and framed, and it hung below the sign that read: *I Live Here.*

Chelle held both of her hands over her mouth as she turned to go back down the hall and found Royce standing right behind her. He pulled her hands down from her mouth and enfolded hers in his.

"Chelle, I just want to make you happy. Right here and right now I want to make you happy."

Chelle fell asleep in his arms that night, and Royce became something that no other man had ever been for her. He didn't try to smother her with kisses and use her vulnerability as an easy road to sex. He simply held her, and for that night he became her sanctuary.

Fifteen days later, Royce and Chelle brought Mattie into his new home. Chelle knew that Royce would help her when he could with the baby because he was falling in love with Mattie in the same way that she had. As soon as his shift ended, he was at the hospital sitting right beside Chelle watching little Mattie sleep. They both couldn't have been more excited if Chelle had given birth to him and Royce had been his father.

They had stopped by Zora's place on the way home, and Zora had cried when she saw Mattie. Chelle was afraid that by the look in Zora's eyes when she held him she would never let him go. Her appearance told Chelle that she was still mourning Mia's death in a major way and that bothered Chelle. She had Mattie and Royce to help her with the grieving process. Zora had Emory, but Chelle knew that Zora needed more to fill the void that her own child had left in her womb. She said a silent prayer for her best friend as she and Royce loaded little Mattie into her car and headed to her own home.

The first place that Chelle had taken Mattie after they entered the apartment was to the wall in his room that held the memory of his mother. And while Royce watched from the bedroom door, Chelle began to tell the child the story of how she was given the chance to become his mother.

ZORA

§

The loneliness that had somehow managed to consume Zora since Mia's death was overwhelming. She didn't want to get out of bed let alone brush her teeth or comb her hair.

When Royce and Chelle had brought the little baby that looked so much like Mia over, it had only reminded her of the fact that Mia had really existed and left a legacy similar to how her empty and barren womb reminded her of Zari.

Life seemed to crawl by, and even though it had only been a few months since Emory left and a couple of weeks since Mia's death, she felt so lonely that she found herself crying a few times a day.

One day when she was sitting on the porch to escape the silence of the house, she heard screams coming from across the street. She didn't even consider going to check on the matter. Her neighbors had so many strange functions in their backyard that there was no telling what was going on. She heard a door slam and saw Karen naked as a jaybird, heading straight for her in a full sprint. Her hair was tousled, and she seemed to be roughed up a bit. Zora rose to her feet and started to ask, "Are you all—"

"You have to hide me!" Karen cut her off before bursting into tears. Zora grabbed the woman instinctively in an embrace and ushered her through her front door.

Once they were safely inside, Zora secured the locks on the door and helped Karen to the couch. She then ran to the linen closet to get a blanket to cover the naked woman's body. She had no idea what was going on, but her first guess was that someone had broken into the house, and Karen was the only one home.

When she returned with the blanket, she handed Karen the phone. She had been quiet after her demand for a hiding place, and Zora hadn't thought to slow down and ask her what was going on. Zora sat on the couch beside the woman, and for the first time she noticed that Karen was strikingly beautiful. Her red hair looked more auburn to Zora up close, and her skin was a toasty tan. Her lips were thin like any other white person's in Zora's opinion, but her blue eyes were striking in contrast with her tanned face.

Zora noticed that Karen was holding the phone, but she wasn't dialing 911. "Do you wanna call the police?" Zora questioned her.

Tears began to slide down Karen's exquisite face, and Zora found herself thinking that she's even pretty when she cries.

"My father told me that *this* life was going to kill me." Her voice had a nice raspy tone, even with the shaking from her tears. "They were so conservative with their fucking beliefs, him and my mother." Zora handed her a tissue from the box that still sat in the center of the coffee table where her mother had kept it.

"I don't believe that though. This life isn't going to kill me." She looked at Zora thoughtfully, and asked, "Will loving a man kill you?"

Zora's eyes widened as she took in the question. She thought about the past few years of her life. She thought about Bryan and how he'd taken something from her so great that at times she thought she'd die. She thought about Will and how he hurt her, but she also thought about the strength and endurance of his wife. Then Emory came into her mind. She smiled without even knowing it. It was her first smile since Mia's passing.

"If you love the wrong man—a loser—I think you can lose a part of yourself. I believe, though, that what doesn't kill you only makes you stronger. Life prepares you for what's next." Zora meant every word. It was in that moment that she knew her losers were preparation for who was really hers. Emory.

Karen was quiet as she reflected on Zora's response. She finally blurted out, "Women can be losers too, you know?" Her lips began to tremble, and an open sob escaped her, "I'm so tired." Zora wrapped her arms around the crying woman and tried to comfort her with trite but genuine phrases like, "let it out" and "it will be OK."

When Karen had calmed down a bit, she continued, "Stacy likes to bring people home and have them do things to me. She likes to watch, and she gets very upset when I say no. It's because I'm not smart like her. I didn't go to college, and I don't make money like she does," She started crying again, but she continued, "She brought four men home today, and she said I had to have all of them. They were holding me down. I was so scared, but I got away."

Zora looked horrified. "Stacy did this to you?" Zora was at a loss for words.

Zora had no idea what to do about the situation. Karen threatened to leave if Zora called the police, so she called Jamie instead. Jamie had always been good at bringing calamity to any situation. She came right over and took control. She talked Karen into going to the police station with her to file a report.

Zora was shocked. She had no idea what had been going on across the street. She shook her head as she thought about how everyone must fall for at least one loser, male or female.

She was relieved when Emory finally called her and told her that he was at the airport. For the first time in a month she felt like she was a part of something for someone. She didn't tell him about Mia's death over the phone, because she deemed it inappropriate. She only smiled and told him that she'd be there soon. She primped and paraded in front of the mirror for as long as she could possibly allow Emory to wait before she finally got into her car and made her way to the airport.

She was anxious as she parked in the underground parking lot, and for almost a whole second she forgot about her pain for Mia and Zari. Emory had been very specific in telling her not to come through the pick-up area. He'd said that he needed her help with the gifts that he had brought her. She had smiled while on the phone, because the last time he returned to the states he'd brought with him all kinds of African treasures. She hadn't removed anything of her parents to hang the beautiful treasures, but she knew that one day soon she would have to part with their things all together and truly move on with her life.

When she entered the airport Zora had to shuffle through all the standard security just to get to where she could wait for Emory. She thought she saw Emory as soon as she had been cleared to stand in the pick-up area. His frame resembled Emory's, and he stood only a few feet away with his back to her. As she walked closer to him and gained a better side view, she knew that she had been mistaken. The man had a baby carrier at his feet and in it sat a tiny newborn baby. Across his chest he wore a harness that held another child that looked to be only a few months older than the newborn. She knew that this man was not Emory.

She looked ahead and kept walking past the man and his children in search of Emory. That is when she heard him. Her name had been called from somewhere behind her.

"Zora," he said again fearing that she had not heard his voice the second time.

Zora turned, and there stood the man with the two children that she had just past. It was him. It was Emory and before she could ask the questions that were beginning to bombard her mind, he spoke.

"Here we are. We've been waiting." He looked down at the baby that was attached to his chest and pointed to Zora.

"I want you to meet your new mother, and I hope, my soon-to-be new wife."

Zora's hand flew to her mouth and she noticed that a few passersby had stopped to watch the emotions that were beginning to transpire.

"Emory," was all that she could choke out, and that seemed to be enough for him. He grabbed the handle to the carrier and walked the ten feet that separated him and Zora.

"Zora, I would like to introduce you to Natilia," he said pointing to the small child on his chest. "I found her in Sudan. She is only three months old." Zora observed the child's dark skin and her hair which held big, black curls. Her cheekbones were extremely high and were the defining factor of the shape of her face. She was beautiful even though all that covered her small body was a dingy white romper.

"Her mother was raped by an Arabic raider from the north, and she was left for dead in the wilderness. She was an orphan when I took her to the camp in Sudan, and she was still an orphan when I went back through for supplies. But today … ," he paused as if he were a bit nervous, "Today—if you say you'll marry me, she'll have a mother and a father." He unsnapped the harness and released the baby, handing her over to Zora. Zora welcomed Natilia into her bosom with open arms while Emory kneeled to the ground where the child in the carrier still slept. Tears formed in her eyes as she rubbed the child's head and watched as Emory lifted the second child.

"Still no 'yes,' huh?" he asked playfully looking up at Zora with the tiny baby in his arms.

"I named her Zari. Today is only her sixth day of life. She is from Ethiopia. Her mother's name was Tausif." Zora's eyebrows went up when she saw the tear that escaped Emory's eye.

"She loved her so much. Before Tausif took her last breath, she asked me to make sure that she always knows that she is loved. She asked me to make sure that I tell her every day that no matter what, God loves her."

He kissed Zari on the top of her head. "I know I can do that. In fact, I can raise both of these little girls to be women on my own, but I think that God wants you to be a part of that. I want you to be part of that." Tears streamed down Zora's face as she stroked Natilia's soft head. All she could think about was how right Pastor Leo had been that day. As Emory spoke to her, she could feel how right this was. She agreed with Emory. This was what she wanted to do, and more than that this was what God wanted her to do.

Still cradling Zari in his arms, Emory freed one of his hands and reached into his pocket. Zora watched curiously as he pulled his hand from his pocket and held up the most beautiful wooden ring that she had ever laid eyes on. It looked to be pure mahogany with small letters carved deeply into it. It was professionally polished and when she held her hand out for him to put it on her finger she saw the tiny "For Zora" that was carved around the outside.

"I can afford to buy you diamonds Zora, but they would never be made just for you. Baby, there is no doubt in my mind that like this ring, you were carved by God just for me. I love you, and no matter what I will always be your friend."

Emory stood up, and with Zari in his arms and Natilia in Zora's, they sank into each other. They stood as a family and listened to the applause of the people from the crowd that had formed earlier watching their meeting.

ONE YEAR LATER

Zora couldn't believe so much time had passed since Mia's death. As she sat at the picnic table and stared out into the yard, she wondered how lives that had been so bad could turn into something so good. She instantly answered her own question with one word: God.

She watched her husband as he chased their beautiful daughter Natilia around Royce and Chelle's backyard. Natilia was stumbling and falling over everything. She had only been walking for a few months, and it showed in her inexperienced stride. She was such a cheerful child. Zora thanked God for both her girls every day.

"You always have them so cute in their matching outfits, Zora," Chelle interrupted her thoughts. She was now sitting across the table with the birthday boy in her lap, and he was sucking on a bottle filled to the rim with milk. Mattie was only a year old, but Zora knew that he would always be a momma's boy. She had been so proud of Chelle when she graduated from law school six months ago and married Royce the same week. He was a good guy, and Zora was happy that he had found Chelle.

"Thank you Chelle, but you know that Mattie cannot be outdone always sporting a new pair of Jordans." They both chuckled as Donisha approached the table.

"I hate to be a party pooper, guys, but you know my husband has to speak tonight." She sighed before adding, "Between me going to school, Ed's baseball, Frankie's dancing, Marcus's speaking engagements, and this one here," she was now holding her stomach between her hands like a basketball and smiling radiantly.

"Yeah, I know, but you look beautiful, Donisha," Chelle responded, "How are things at the church, by the way? I mean how are people receiving Marcus's story? I know it was kinda hard for ya'll in the beginning."

Donisha's face brightened even more as she began, "It was hard at first, ya'll. I didn't think my husband would make it through the emotional slander that they were dragging him through, but God always has a plan. Last month when he spoke at the Young Men's Conference in Dallas, fifty young men came to the altar asking for prayer because they too had been raped at some point in their lives and were feeling confused."

"Praise the Lord," Chelle and Zora replied in unison, and all three girls shared a laugh.

As their laughter died down, Donisha looked over at her two friends and said in a dazed tone, "We have changed, huh?"

"And that's a good thing," Kyla said approaching them from behind with a huge birthday gift bag in her hand.

"Hey girl," Chelle said in a cheery voice, "Where's Peter?"

Kyla waved her hand over toward where Peter stood with Emory and Natilia on the other side of the yard.

"You know he had to go find Em, he can't wait until next week when they leave for Thailand. I don't know who's more excited about this adoption, him or the child."

Zora looked up at Kyla from her seat at the table and said, "Well, Kyla, you guys are doing a great thing. It's not every day that a child is saved from that type of environment. Em was so distraught after they rescued him. Just imagine a child in a brothel at the age of six, and his parents were the ones that sold him into prostitution. When Kenu tested positive for HIV, Em called home crying. I told him that HIV didn't mean it was the end of the child's life. He said that without the proper medicine and care, he knew that the boy's condition would worsen to AIDS as quickly as Zari's birth mother, and then he really would die. That's when I called you," Zora smiled at Kyla, "I knew you and Peter were having problems adopting here because of Peter's condition, and I knew that you would love Kenu no matter what."

Kyla laughed and gently slapped Zora on the back. "You and your husband are always trying to save the world. It was the most difficult process in the world. Lord have mercy, though, we made it through. After all the screening and digging in our business them folks did, I thought they'd surely stamp a giant 'no' on our application packet as soon as they found out about Peter and his HIV." She smiled wide, "They didn't though, and in a few weeks someone will be calling ya girl mama."

Zora laughed and said, "Hey, with this world we live in, anything is worth a try. Anyway, has anyone seen Jamie?" she asked looking around the table at her friends.

Donisha interjected when she saw Marcus and the kids standing by the fence waiting for her. "Sorry guys, I gotta go, but are we still on for The Den this week?"

"You know it," Zora said, answering for them all as Donisha waved good-bye and disappeared through the gate that led out of out of Chelle's backyard.

"No, actually," Kyla began, "I haven't seen Jamie, but you know my new patient Charles?" Zora and Chelle nodded their heads in unison. "Well he was trying to tell me that he saw her at a strip club all hugged up with a woman. Charles has only seen her with me a few times, so I told him he had to be mistaken. Shoot, I hope he was mistaken. If I know Jamie, she's just somewhere enjoying some real good church.

Zora looked toward the patio door when she heard a faint cry come from inside. She jumped from her seat and rushed over to the open door to see Zari standing in the playpen where she had been peacefully sleeping before. She picked Zari up and kissed her cheek.

Zora loved both of the girls equally, but just as Natilia was a daddy's girl, Zari was Zora's. Zora rubbed the fine patch of sand-colored hair that sat on top of her daughter's mostly bald head and smiled. Since the day that Emory had introduced Zari to her, Zora had been intrigued by the child's majestic look. Her face had held such defining features for a child so young. Zora envied her perfectly shaped lips and the pinkness that they held. They looked as if an artist had drawn them with precision. Her chestnut-colored skin was as flawless as any baby's, and Zora always smiled at how she could have easily been her birth mother.

Zari's HIV test had come back negative every time she had been tested since she arrived in America, and Zora knew that God had something to do with that.

She walked into Chelle's kitchen and got Zari's strained food from the large storage bag that she always carried with her. "I'll bet mommy's little angel is hungry. Let's get you something to eat, little girl."

Zari smiled as she nuzzled into Zora chest. "I love you too," Zora whispered as she walked out onto the patio and was greeted by her husband and daughter.

"Hey," he began with the same twinkle in his eye that had been there the day they met. "We were just on our way in to tell you that Natilia here is getting a bit cranky. I'm gonna walk her down to the house with me to get Peter some information about our trip and let Gideon out for a potty break. I think she'll be fine if I get her outta here for a while. That may be all she needs." Zora nodded her head at him, and he bent down and first kissed Zari on the cheek and then Zora on her lips.

As Emory pushed the stroller and he disappeared from the backyard with Natilia and Peter, Zora smiled. Her life had become such a blessing that she had been able to be a blessing to someone else.

Zora and Emory married two weeks after his proposal, and after the wedding, she put her parents' house up for sale. She had known that is was time for her to move on. And because of her daughters and new husband, she was more than ready to do it. The house was on the market for approximately two days before Chelle voiced her interest in purchasing it. Her parents had been asking her what she wanted as a graduation gift, and she'd known that she wanted to provide her son with a home. Zora and Emory sold the house to Chelle and grew very close to Chelle and Royce as a family.

Zora's old neighbor Stacy put her house up for sale after Karen left and didn't return to her. Peter and Kyla would be closing on that house in three days, and they were anxious to get it ready for their new child.

Zora walked back over to the picnic table where Chelle was still sitting as she watched Kyla push Mattie on the swing set that Royce had bought when they first bought the house.

She sat down with Zari on her lap and began to remove the lids of the containers of her strained carrots, peas, and chicken. When she looked up across the table, Chelle stared at her with a big bright smile.

"I don't know what God saw in us, Zora. We were a bunch of losers, and look at what he did in our lives. He loved us when we couldn't even love ourselves."

Zora eyed her thoughtfully and then smiled herself, "That's just the God he is, Chelle. I found out through all that mess that I went through, you went through, Donisha, and everybody else, that losers come in all shapes and sizes, sexes, and shades. Shoot, you're right. We were even losers ourselves, and God still loves us. He made us in his image, and that's exactly what we were: in love with losers."

ABOUT THE AUTHOR

LaToya S. Watkins, a Dallas native, has been reading and writing as far back as her memory carries her. She received her B.A. in Literary Studies from the University of Texas at Dallas (UTD). She is currently enrolled in a Masters program at Southern Methodist University. She has been published in *Thought* magazine as a contest winner, *Work.com* and the *North Dallas Gazette,* as a freelance writer, and *TWINS* magazine as a contributor. She has also worked as an editor at the Schlager Group Inc., in Dallas, Texas. LaToya resides in Plano, Texas, with her husband, three children, and three dogs. She is currently working on her second book, *Dorothy.* Visit the author online at www.LaToyaSWatkins.com.

In *Love* with Losers

Ordering Information

Yes! Please send me ________ copies of
In Love with Losers.

Please include $15.00 plus $3.00 shipping/handling for the first book and $1.00 for each additional book.

Send my book(s) to:
Name:____
Address:______________________________________
City, State,
Zip:____
Telephone:____________________________________
Email:____

Would you like to receive emails from
Peace In The Storm Publishing?
____Yes _____No

Peace In The Storm Publishing, LLC.
Attn: Book Orders
P.O. Box 1152
Pocono Summit, PA 18346
www.PeaceInTheStormPublishing.com

LaVergne, TN USA
29 March 2010

177470LV00002B/45/P